I0830414

DEADLY
OBSESSION
GRAYTON D.

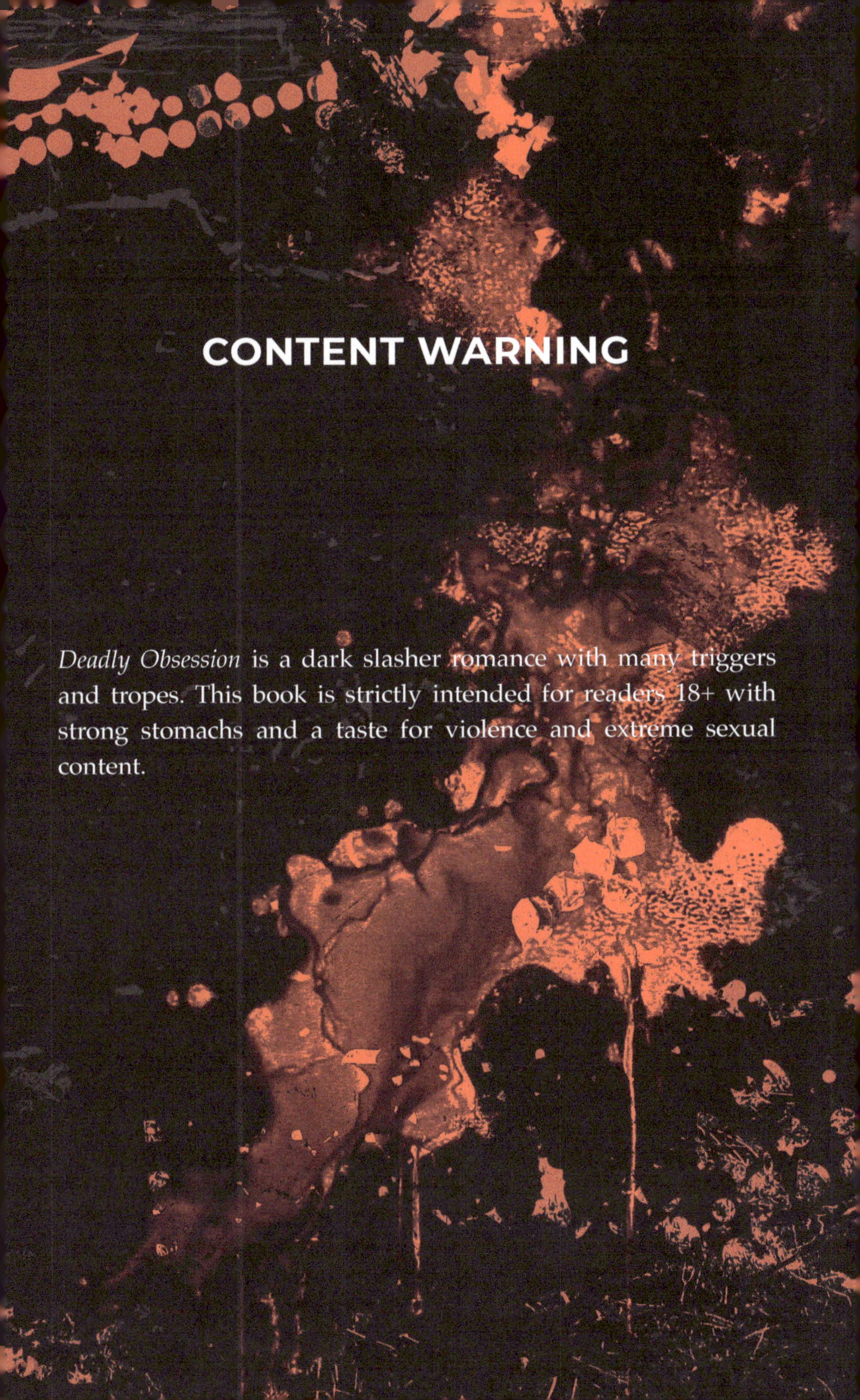

CONTENT WARNING

Deadly Obsession is a dark slasher romance with many triggers and tropes. This book is strictly intended for readers 18+ with strong stomachs and a taste for violence and extreme sexual content.

TRIGGER WARNINGS

CNC; Axe/knife play
Blood play
Bondage
Hunting
Rough/sadism (choking/spanking/slapping/impact play)
Degradation/praise/worship
Orgasm control
Sensory deprivation
Implied rape
Sexual assault
Drowning
Dismemberment
Drugging (non-con)
Mention of past miscarriage
Stalking
Graphic murder
Murder of law enforcement
Masked men
Service members suffering from PTSD

Mental health representation (schizophrenia)
Suicide
Graphic scenes depicting battles from the war in Afghanistan
Brief mention of use of children suicide bombers in Afghanistan
Implied cheating
Intoxicated sexual encounter
Golden shower (non-con)
Mention of sibling death
Maternal mortality
Somnophilia (her on him)
Parent-on-child emotional abuse/neglect
Psychological abuse
Mention of possible necrophilia
"What really is happily ever after?"

DEDICATION

For my fellow deranged readers who grew up realizing the sexual tension in films like Scream, Friday the 13th, and Halloween and have forever felt shortchanged. The masked, erotic, dark slasher story you've desired is here. Be careful what you wish for.

PLAYLIST

Bodies: Drowning Pool (Author's pick for the overall title)
Face Down: The Red Jumpsuit Apparatus
The Game: WWE Motorhead
S&M: Sabl3
Pretty Little Poison: Warren Zeiders
She Will Be Loved: Maroon 5
Jekyll and Hyde: Five Finger Death Punch
Sin So Sweet: Warren Zeiders
Die MF Die: Dope
A Bar Song: Shaboozey
Spin You Around (1/24): Morgan Wallen (James & Sera's Dance)
Eyes on Fire: Blue Foundation
Barbie Girl: Sabl3 (Lyndsey's song)
Call A Cowboy: Lainey Wilson
Lips like Morphine: Kill Hannah
Nightmare: Avenged Sevenfold
Goddess: Written by Wolves
Beg!: Vana
Helena: My Chemical Romance

Wrong Side of Heaven: Five Finger Death Punch
Psycho: Hardy
Monster: Skillet
girls girls girls: Fletcher
Afterlife: Avenged Sevenfold
I Get Off: Halestorm
Lullaby: The Spill Canvas
One Step Closer: Linkin Park
The American Nightmare: Ice Nine Kills
Gone Country: Thomas Rhett (Bonus Sera & James's song)

EPIGRAPHS

"Words have no power to impress the mind without the exquisite horror of their reality."
   - Edgar Allan Poe

"I'm sure that in time, every bit of her will be gone and her death will be a mystery... even to me."
   - Stephen King, *Two Past Midnight: Secret Window, Secret Garden*

PROLOGUE

Around the time I'd finally decided to leave my husband, one of my girlfriends gifted me two things that would change my life forever: a vibrator and the novel *God of Malice* by Rina Kent. Since then, I hadn't gone a single day without an orgasm, along with a fantasy about masked, muscular, tattooed American men.

Thank you, Kearsten.

1

SERA

As the Uber slowed to a stop, the gravel of the dirt road crunching beneath the tires, I took in the scene before me through my window. The moon was full in the night sky, providing a sparse sheet of light on the towering trees that swayed in the autumn's chilling breeze. The cabin seemed to appear out of nowhere, the faint twinkling lights I'd spotted through the dense forest minutes earlier rapidly taking the form of a warmly-illuminated front porch.

The two-story rustic cabin was exactly as advertised on the Airbnb website. A slight glow from the main floor windows along with the porch lights cut away small sections of the night, revealing a portion of the surrounding area as I stepped out of the car. To one side of the home was a stone patio with multiple pieces of furniture and a large fire pit. Somewhere beyond the house, I could hear the gentle flow of water, likely the creek I'd seen in the photos.

Shutting my car door and retrieving my luggage from the

trunk, I then wished the driver farewell and he departed. The chill night air softly stung the exposed skin on my face and neck, a sharp contrast to the warmth of the automobile. I walked with purpose up the long set of stairs to the front porch, punched in the code on the electronic lock box just beside the ring camera, drew out the key, and opened the door. The soothing scent of pumpkin spice mixed with the old natural wood of the cabin drew me in, instantly putting my body at ease.

This was exactly what I needed: a peaceful night alone in the middle of nowhere. No one else was expected to arrive until Sunday afternoon. For one night, it was just me, TikTok, and my fantasy book boyfriends. Tonight's flavor: Ryat.

Stepping into the cabin, I locked the door behind me. Then I began to survey the room just as the old grandfather clock rang out. The strained sound of the escapement mechanism's many aged gears and cogs—in need of lubrication—gave the likely once-beautiful chime an eerie undertone. My eyes locked on to the old clock across the room just as the fifth chime sounded and suddenly all the lights went out. A loud *thud* boomed from beneath my feet, vibrating the wooden floor. My body tensed and my pulse quickened. I'd always been afraid of the dark.

"Shit… Hello? Is someone here?"

The clock continued its eerie marking of the hour, each clang making me flinch. Turning, I frantically searched for the door knob, finding it by the final chime and right when the lights snapped back on. I froze, cleared my throat, and turned back around while forcing out a tremulous laugh. The cabin was built in the 1920s and, in the middle of the woods, there were bound to be some electrical problems. That *thud* was probably just a possum or something scared off by my arrival.

"Get it together, Sera Watson," I said out loud, mocking my mother's voice.

Remembering the floor plan and which room I'd been

assigned, I headed upstairs to the main suite with my things and made myself at home.

Fifteen minutes later, I was sitting on the large couch in the great room, in my pajamas. With the fireplace going, the lights dimmed and a glass of chardonnay, I settled in with *The Ritual* by Shantel Tessier.

Hello, Ryat Archer.

Just as I was getting back to the world of Ryat and Blakely, my phone's Discord notification sounded with a new message. A smile pulled at the corners of my lips when I saw who it was from.

JAMES

> Hey, beautiful. Welcome to America.
> Have a nice flight?

ME

> Hey, you. Yeah, long but not bad.
> Already at the cabin. I was just about to
> sit down and read before heading
> to bed.

JAMES

> Oh, yeah, how is it? Still on The Ritual?

ME

> The cabin is beautiful. It was already
> dark out when I arrived so I haven't seen
> the outside too much, but I love it so far!
> Can't wait for all of you to get here. And
> yes, still reading The Ritual. It's so good.
> So hot!

I couldn't help smiling at my phone like an idiot at the use of the pet name he'd given me—Harpy. He'd first used it when I'd told him about the day I left my abusive ex-husband. Mike had attempted to grab me and prevent me from leaving the home, and in response, I turned and slashed my freshly-done nails across his face. When the cuts finally healed, he'd been left with two long, thin scars from above his brow to his nose. James had found not only amusement in my story, but he'd told me he was both impressed and proud of me. And that was when he'd called me *a ravishing harpy.*

Suddenly, I found myself scrolling up in our messages on Discord. James aka "Mustang" and I had been teasing each other for months, even more so since this trip was planned. We'd started with descriptive messages and audio clips, then evolved to photos and video messages, our lust getting the better of us. At this point, we'd seen practically every inch of each other's bodies, with the exception of the mask-covered lower halves of our faces. Which only added petrol to the lust-fueled fire.

I'd read many dark romance books over the last year, and every time I'd picked up another one, it unlocked something within me. I discovered a new kink I thought I might never get to explore. *Like a thing for masked men.*

Over the last year, I'd been part of an actively growing community on TikTok and Discord called "The Red Room." To celebrate one full year, a special meet-and-greet vacation had been planned and a location had been randomly selected. Shingletown, located in Northern California and surrounded by the state's famous sequoia pines and cedars, was one of the most secluded and beautiful destinations optioned. The plan was for all available members to meet on the second Sunday of October and stay until the following Saturday.

Closing the messages with James, I opened my text thread with my parents and smiled at the photos of Alex they'd sent me earlier. My parents, excited for me to be getting away and taking some time for myself, not only agreed to watch their grandson but also purchased my plane tickets. Of course, I was grateful. At the same time, it meant I was at their mercy when it came to scheduling. I quickly learned they had me arriving at 7pm on the Saturday evening prior to the Airbnb reservation. Fortunately, voicing my problem to the other eight members who would be attending the trip quickly resulted in the property owners agreeing to let me show up a night early.

This would be the longest I'd been away from my parents in years, and the first time I'd ever been away from Alexander longer than the occasional sleepover at his best mate's house. Alexander had been exposed to things a child should never have been exposed to within his early years. Neither of us should have been.

My mind began slipping down that dangerous slope to the horrible memories I'd been trying so hard to block out. I missed my parents. But most of all, right now, I missed my son.

Opening my camera, I switched it from photo to video, flipped to selfie mode and pressed record. "Hey, baby boy! Mummy just wanted to say I love you so very much and I'll be home before you know it! Be extra good for grandma and grandpa!"

I dropped the video in the text string and hit send before closing it and looking at my home screen. Smiling, I kissed the photo of my baby boy I used as my background wallpaper. Then I turned off the screen and picked up my book, trying to distract myself from the horrid memories. Something I found difficult enough in my consciousness and impossible to contain in the dream world. Before long, though, I felt the familiar heaviness of fatigue weighing on my eyes. And with book in hand, I sank into the darkness.

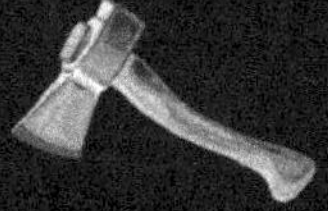

"There's Daddy's Sera Doll! Daddy is home and so horny," he said, his words slurring as he stumbled forward. I could hear Alexander crying in the distance, clearly woken by his father's abrupt entrance into our bedroom.

Standing from our bed, I went to move past my husband, only to be stopped by a large hand on my shoulder, the other gripping my breast through my pajama top.

"Mike, let me go. Alexander is crying," I pleaded softly.

"Fucking brat can wait! Shut up, kid!" he said, still gripping me as he yelled at our son. His breath reeked of cheap whiskey, and I could see lipstick stains on his neck and what looked like bite marks.

"Mike, let—" was all I could get out before I felt the back of his hand come across my face, and I saw stars.

"Shut up, bitch," he barked and shoved me back, my legs catching on the frame and causing me to fall onto the bed. Then I watched in horror as he staggered towards me, undoing his trousers as my child's cries echoed from down the hall.

2

SERA

My eyes snapped open, rescuing me from the nightmare that had become a recurring one, more and more since Mike had started leaving terrifying things near my and my parents' home. The constables couldn't or *wouldn't* do anything, saying that technically we had no proof it was him. I was living in a nightmare that never ended, far worse than Freddy Krueger because my boogeyman pursued me in and out of my dreams. It had gotten to the point my mind had started conjuring up some very permanent solutions to my misery—solutions of the darkest kind.

Shaking my head and rubbing my eyes, I found myself still lying on the couch. "Damn..." I cursed under my breath as I rubbed at my stiff neck.

The lights were all off but the flames from the mammoth hearth did a good job of illuminating the majority of the room. Looking around, I spotted my glass of wine on the end table behind me, right where I left it.

But where was my book?

I searched the couch and the floor and I still couldn't see it anywhere. Standing up to ensure I was not sitting on it, I happened to glance over to the fireplace and froze as I struggled to process the changes in the room. Not only were there fresh logs in the fire, but propped up on the mantle just below the television was my book.

"How the fuck…" I whispered softly to myself as I stepped closer.

Picking up the book, I noticed my bookmark sticking out from between the pages. I opened it up and instantly recognized the scene that had been marked. I'd already read the chapter—the one where Blakeley had a dream about the masked man chasing her. It was my favorite, something only a handful of people knew.

One of the logs on the fire shifted in front of me, the noise and the flicker of light causing me to jump and slam the book closed. "Shit!" I cried out, taking a step back.

Before I had a moment to catch my breath, I *caught* sight of something else in my periphery. I turned on my heel, my eyes locking on an imposing figure, the dark silhouette lost in the night's void. All except his mask. Black. One side smooth and faceless, a red slash cutting across the hollow eye socket, and the other shaped like a human skull.

But it was the white of the figure's eyes glaring at me that had time freezing as I watched him slowly slide the door open and step into the room. He was dressed in all-black tactical clothing with a bundle of black rope attached to his hip. He appeared to be well over six-feet tall and athletically built, a wall of horrifying darkness. Not a sliver of skin was exposed; the only part of him I could see was the light-green color of his irises, and they were honed in on me.

Taking a few more steps in my direction, he stopped at the halfway mark. Then, with unblinking eyes, he slowly growled out, "Run."

As if that one word had pried my feet from where they were

cemented to the floor, I took off like a shot. The problem was, I had no idea where I was or where to go. All I knew was that I had to get *away*.

Bolting out the front double doors, I turned left and ran down the hill that led to the lower half of the split-level house. As I passed the entrance, I heard the thudding stomps of boots on the wooden deck above me. Then, as though he were in some supervillain movie, the masked man landed heavily in a crouch position on the ground before me with a grunt.

My heels skidded to a halt, my body instinctively leaning away and causing me to fall backwards onto my ass. Screaming, I turned and pushed off the dirt with as much energy as I could force out with the adrenaline flooding into my numb limbs.

"Help!" I cried out as I sprinted down the gravel driveway, which must have taken twenty minutes to navigate in the Uber and I didn't recall seeing any homes or even lights for miles before that.

Behind me, I could hear the crunching of the man's boots as he kept pace with me. There was no way I was going to get much farther in nothing but my pajamas and house slippers— along with the thousands of tiny rocks, I could also feel the occasional stick stabbing at the bottom of my feet. Hoping for softer ground, I cut sharply off the driveway to enter the woods. Maybe I could lose him among the dense trees and make it back to the cabin to call for help…

Fuck, I wish I had my phone. Did the cabin even have a landline?

My thoughts raced as I continued my frantic run through the woods in no particular direction. I pushed past twisting branches and pointed twigs from the various trees and underbrush, even as they cut through my silk pajamas. I was fairly certain I was bleeding from more than one superficial wound. The chilled fall air felt like shards of glass, growing sharper in my chest.

Daring to glance over a shoulder, I allowed a faint wave of relief to wash over me. He was gone. *I'd lost him!*

I came to an abrupt stop, resting one hand on my heart and the other on my knee as I doubled over, attempting to calm my ragged breathing. Then I hauled myself upright and turned. Stepping without looking before I crashed right into that mountain of a nightmare. All muscle and slitted, menacing eyes.

"Tag, you're mine," he said with a low growl that quickly turned into a dark, rumbling laugh.

With my heart lodged in my throat, I spun on my heel as quickly as I could to put distance between us. But within a few short strides, I heard a faint whistle from behind me. A split second later, I caught the glint of something flying over my head before sinking itself into the tree directly in front of me with a loud crack.

A fucking axe! Great, not only was I being chased by a horrifying masked man, he was a bloody axe murderer too!

My moment's hesitation cost me any ground I had gained, the muffled breathing of the masked man growing closer and closer as I turned to accept my fate. I looked up into his eyes, tears running down my face, but I couldn't make a sound. His gloved hand reached up and closed around my throat, his heavy steps forcing me backwards till I was pressed against the tree.

My gut was telling me to fight back, to claw at his face, but that was impossible with his mask on. Daring a moment to look him up and down, I confirmed what I already knew. There wasn't an inch of exposed skin, and while I considered myself a capable woman, I was not overpowering this man—this monster.

With one hand still clenching my throat, he pulled something from his belt. "Wrists out in front," he growled, leaving no room for hesitation.

I obeyed, slowly holding out my trembling hands towards

him. Afraid if I reached out too far, I might be figuratively burned by the hellfire staring back at me. Before I knew it, rope was being wrapped around my wrists, my entire body flinching at the feel of it pressing into my skin. A small gasp escaped my lips, his right hand never leaving my throat as he gripped the makeshift cuffs by the center and raised my hands up over my head.

My shoulders strained as he continued to extend my arms just past my reach, so that I had to lift myself onto my toes to accommodate how high he demanded my body go. Daring to look up where he gripped the rope, I watched as he hooked the center of it onto the top of the axe head protruding from the tree at the perfect angle.

There was no hope of me getting free.

"That's my good girl," he said, patting my cheek with his now-free hand, then took a step back, his eyes scanning over me like I was a meal.

At those words of praise, my body betrayed my good senses. I should have been terrified, screaming, fighting, but this was like my darkest fantasy. Right out of my book.

Fuck, this monster knew it… And was I hallucinating or did his voice sound familiar?

Somehow he'd put my bookmark on the exact page where Blakley had dreamed about something very similar.

I looked up into the eyes of my masked predator and saw emerald irises burning into mine. Suddenly, despite his hand not being around my throat anymore, I could breathe even less. The only sound I could register was his deep, heavy, long pants. Like a lustful monster restraining itself.

"Looks like I've caught myself a harpy," he said in a low, gravelly but honey-sweet voice.

"James…" The name escaped from my lips as recognition dawned on me.

My chest grew tight as I awaited confirmation of my suspicion. None came but only one person had ever called me that. My core heated as memories of past conversations flooded my mind. Late night exchanges of words and photos as we teased and pleased each other.

Stepping back into me, my masked captor drew another small axe from a holster hanging from his belt and turned it slowly, its edge catching the moonlight so that it seemed to sparkle. His free hand reached out and gripped the bottom of my blouse as he tugged it towards him, my eyes fixating on the tip of the blade dipping closer to my throat.

My shoulders were burning, my body instinctively leaning away from the axe, despite the bark of the tree already stabbing through my blouse. I watched in silent horror—and excitement—as he gently placed the tip of the blade to the collar seam of my blouse and slowly glided it down the center, parting my pajama top like butter. The cold air intensified over my bare chest, causing my nipples to harden to stone.

With my chest exposed to him, he tilted his head side to side, taking in my breasts as if he were judging them like some piece of art in an exhibit. He raised the axe in front of my face and my eyes caught on the tip, pink fibers from my blouse hanging from a chip in its edge. My entire body tensed in anticipation of what I was certain was coming next.

Then I felt the gloved fingers of his free hand caressing the side of my face again, slowly moving down my neck and over my breasts while my gaze remained locked on the blade and those fibers. He took his time brushing each of my peaked nipples with his knuckles. The sensation sending a warm rush through my entire body.

My tunnel vision on the axe blade broke off as he flipped it in his hand so that the head was against his forearm, the blade towards me before it disappeared as he lowered the handle between us. Until all I could see was a pair of unblinking, predator-like green eyes glaring at me through the narrow slits of his mask. The axe brushed against my leg, and both his thumbs hooked on to the waistline of my pajama bottoms as he forced them down past my hips till they fell freely to the forest floor.

"No panties? Hmmmm," he seemed to growl as his empty hand made its slow and exploratory journey back up my body, his gloved fingertips leaving a trail of heat I couldn't explain. I shuddered when something smooth and hard glided over my pussy. "And already dripping wet." That gravelly voice came out low, almost praise-like.

At that, I looked down and realized I was grinding against the handle of his axe! *Oh my God, Sera, you are seriously fucked in the head.* But I couldn't stop myself. It felt too good, and he knew it.

He leaned in close and I heard him take in a deep inhale. "I love vanilla," he said under his breath, clearly picking up the scent of my favorite shampoo.

He quickened the pace, pressing the belly of the handle harder, enough to barely hurt as he slid it up and down while I continued to grind against it like an animal in heat.

Just when I was about to orgasm, though, the bastard stopped. And with his free hand reaching up and closing around my throat, he said, "No, baby girl, *I'm* going to make you come. Just me. If you move those sinful hips of yours one inch, I'll stop. Understand?"

I nodded my head, wishing he would keep going already.

His thumb broke from my throat and brushed over my lower lip, dragging the skin down with the action. "Manners. That's *yes, Sir*. Try it."

His hand eased around my throat the slightest bit, allowing me to breathe easier, and I managed to let out a soft, "Yes, Sir," before he closed it tighter once more.

"Now, that's my good girl," he growled out as he resumed

the back-and-forth motion. This time, though, I couldn't tell what was brushing over my pussy lips. He parted them with ease, the wood well-lubricated from my arousal as he slid the first two inches of the axe handle into me.

I let out a restrained gasp and my eyes searched once more for his. I found them immediately. They were still locked on to me as if he were ready to sink his fangs into my neck like a starved vampire. Desire had me fighting the urge to buck into the handle, but the knowledge that he would edge me each time I did granted me a measure of control.

Growing closer once more to an orgasm, I moaned as his gloved thumb joined in, rubbing at my clit in small circles as he fucked me with the axe. My breathing got heavier with each movement, the chilled night air freezing my lungs.

"Hush…" he whispered as he cut off my means to breathe. It seemed the tighter his hand got around my throat, the faster he fucked me, and the closer I came to a climax. I was seeing stars, my vision blurring and my entire body tingling with the fire of sexual desire this stranger had engulfed me in.

"Come for me. Let it go. Let it all go," I heard him say, and that was all it took.

My core erupted, my legs shaking as I came harder on this stranger's axe and thumb than I'd ever done in my entire life. His hand eased its grip on my throat as I gasped. My body continued to tremble, and I found myself suddenly grateful that I was hooked up against this tree. My legs were certainly incapable of supporting me right now.

"Now that's a good girl, Sera, such a good girl," he praised as he slowly drew his axe handle out and raised it to my face, maintaining eye contact as he rested the end on my lower lip.

I could smell the sweet scent of my arousal. Opening wide, I allowed him to slide it inside before wrapping my lips around the wood as I sucked and licked myself off the smooth surface.

My mouth made a popping noise as he drew it back again, my eyes still locked on to his as I stretched my tongue out to give the axe one last lick.

What the fuck was I doing?

There was a good chance this was my fantasy masked-man Mustang, but I didn't know for sure, did I? In this moment, I wasn't certain I cared. I couldn't remember the last time I'd ever gotten off with another person, and I'd never wanted it more—no matter how wrong it might have been.

He raised the axe between us as he seemed to admire it approvingly, turning it from side to side in front of my face. I noticed the way the metal glistened, a single drop of liquid slowly running down the blade's edge.

"You're simply feral for it, aren't you, baby girl?" His eyes focused on my arousal running down the tip, and I could hear the smile from under his mask without ever having to see it. "Lick it off," he said in a commanding tone that allowed no opportunity for argument.

Leaning forward, I slowly stuck out my tongue and licked the axe from the blade's heel up to the toe. The sweetness of my arousal blended with the sting and warm, thick copper taste and I knew I'd just cut my tongue as blood started to fill my mouth and smear across my lower lip.

He cocked his arm back and I flinched, pulling myself against the tree while trying to get as low as I could. The axe head came down, the sound of metal on wood telling me he'd stuck the blade into the bark above me.

I opened my eyes and peered up to see for myself, but his gloved hand gripped my chin as he lifted the bottom of his mask, revealing a well-trimmed beard. Then he closed the distance, pressing his lips to mine, his tongue lashing out and licking my bottom lip before I opened my own mouth. Our tongues met in a hot and bloody, passionate kiss.

Just as quickly as he was there, though, he was gone. He

pulled his mask back down and was looking me over. "So fucking sweet," he said, as his hands dropped to his waist.

At the sound of Velcro ripping apart, I looked down to see he'd unfastened his tactical belt and trousers. I watched in fascination *and mild fear* as he slid his trousers and briefs down his tattooed thighs. My jaw dropped as his hard length sprung out like a starved beast uncaged. I'd seen a fair number of cocks in my life, mostly in pornos sadly, but this one was either the largest of them all or quite on par with the biggest I'd seen.

He stood there for a moment, stroking himself, and I could feel his eyes scanning over every inch of me. Then, reaching down between my legs, he lifted me into the air so that I was straddling him as he pressed my back harder against the bark of the tree. The pain didn't quite register over the drowning lust in my core. I wanted this man to take me in every way imaginable, and I trusted that he would.

With one arm hooked under my leg, he guided the tip of his cock to my now-drenched pussy. Slowly brushing his tip over it like a paint brush preparing to create a masterpiece, coating himself in my wetness.

My lips parted and the word escaped before my mind had a moment to think otherwise. "Please…"

"Please what, Sera…?"

"Please fuck me…" My eyes caught on the burning forest-greens of my masked man as he answered my plea that came out more as a prayer.

I felt his tip breach me, felt every inch of him sink deeper and deeper, till his cock was buried to the hilt. His body pressed against mine, the bark biting into my skin. And I loved it.

My mouth dropped open, a sharp exhale releasing in the form of steam in the chilled night air as he took me. My entire body tensed, the strain on my arms now forgotten as this masked man set me on fire from the inside. My legs tightened around him, denying him the option of retreat. We were past the point of no return, and he was my Phantom. I needed this, as fucked as it was.

He began at a slow pace. It was almost gentle, caring. But with each thrust, I could hear his breathing deepen as he began to pump up into me harder.

"Fuck, Harps..." he groaned, the forehead of his mask digging into my cheek so that I could feel the warmth of his breath escaping from underneath it.

One of his arms left my leg briefly as he reached up to the chin of his mask, tilting it up and back. I attempted to turn my head to catch a glimpse of his face, hoping to confirm my suspicions, but I was denied as that same hand then closed around my neck. His palms were massive and covered the entirety of the front of my throat, yet still allowed him the reach to push my jaw to the side with his thumb. I felt the warm, soft sensation of full lips against my neck. Followed by a consuming, lustful bite as the masked man sank his teeth into my neck.

My body, already at his mercy, became feral in that moment. Using every bit of my energy to ride his cock to nirvana. My treacherous hips bucked, trying to match each of his thrusts as I inched closer and closer to the edge of another orgasm. An orgasm I needed, deserved, and craved. If there was any chance that I was going to die tonight, I was going to do it satisfied.

"Come for me. Let go."

My legs quaked, my body tensed, and my jaw went slack, as I obeyed and my orgasm came over me like a wave crashing on the shore. Every muscle strained and relaxed repeatedly as my pussy gripped him inside me. My shoulder blades pushed off the tree, forcing my hips against him. He didn't falter. Instead, he pressed harder up into me with another brutal thrust. The assault on my sensitive clit was more than I could endure as I impaled myself on his throbbing length.

As I came apart on his cock, his teeth vibrated against my skin, the heat of his breath increasing with his moan. Then he erupted deep inside me, the sudden shot of warmth on my core surprising and pleasurable. My body instinctively tightening around him as if milking him for every drop.

We each relaxed, my eyes growing heavy as he adjusted himself, before my vision went black.

3

JAMES

Once I had Sera unhooked from the tree, I untied her wrists and retrieved my tomahawk. Putting her over my shoulder before I started back towards the cabin.

After we'd both gotten off, she'd passed out from what I could only assume to be the adrenaline crash, the release of so much sexual tension and extreme exhaustion—*it'd be early morning where she was from right now.*

Once inside, I locked the front door behind me and took her upstairs to the main bedroom initially reserved for her and one of the other girls—a change I'd already arranged with Lyndsey, our designated travel planner.

When I'd first found out Sera would be arriving early, I'd started putting the entire plan together. I'd known from the start that her best friend in the Discord, Danielle, would likely offer to arrive early as well so that Sera wouldn't be alone. So, naturally, I'd had to fill Danielle in on my idea so that she wouldn't show up and spoil things. She couldn't have been more pleased to assist; though I don't think she was too thrilled about giving up the main suite.

Oh well.

Placing Sera down across the bed gently, I paused for a moment, unable to pull my eyes away from her elegant form. The woman I'd begun falling for months ago, from a different time zone, was right here in front of me. Her black hair lying loosely on the bed over her shoulders, her exposed breasts even more amazing in person than I had dreamed. Every inch of her was better than I'd imagined.

Were she awake right now and able to hear my thoughts, surely she'd argue about her hair or claim that the faint tiger stripes she'd earned from becoming a mother made her less than perfect. And to that, I'd tell her she was mad.

Smirking, I shook my head at the fake conversation I'd just played out in my mind and stepped off towards the bathroom.

I'd already been at the house for hours, setting a few things up before I saw Sera's Uber come down the road. I'd hidden my truck off near the tree line by the large stream, knowing it wouldn't be seen from the driveway especially in the night.

Stepping over to the large copper freestanding tub, I ran the water and dropped in a bath bomb before turning to move back to the bedroom. I caught a glimpse of myself in the mirror and paused. I was dressed head to toe in black tactical gear with a mask that looked as if it came right out of one of her favorite books. It wasn't terribly different from the aesthetic I'd put on my own TikTok videos, but it was certainly more military. More intimidating too.

Pulling the mask off my head, I turned it in my hands, taking in the paint job I'd given it to make it more unique, more terrifying, while leaving my eyes the focus. I set it on the bathroom counter, crossed back into the bedroom, and stripped down to my briefs, dropping my clothing into the dirty clothes hamper. Then I walked towards the bed and smiled down at Sera as I carefully removed what remained of her pajamas, scooped her up into my tattooed arms, and carried her into the bathroom.

Stopping just before the tub when our joint reflection in the mirror caught my eye this time, and I paused to take in the sight.

It was almost poetic. She looked so small and delicate. Her fair, slightly sun-kissed skin decorated with the occasional fine-line tattoo, an elegant contrast to my fur-covered chest, the majority of my body forever marked with a mix of scars and ink.

Looking at her, my mind drifted back to how it all began in December of last year.

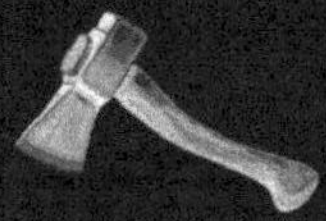

I'd been at the social media thing for a little over a year by then, built up a decent following, and made a handful of good friends. After a long day outside mending fences and tending to the herd, I was worn down to the core. By the time I'd stumbled into my own one-bedroom home on my family's ranch, it was a wonder I'd had the energy to even rinse off in the shower before getting in bed.

Pulling a Budweiser from the mini-fridge that doubled as a night-stand, I popped the top, letting the cap fall to the floor, and grabbed my laptop. My family had no idea about my secret online life as "Mustang." They wouldn't understand it one bit.

My parents were very old-school, southern-Baptist ranchers, just like their parents before them, and theirs before that, and so on and so on. I was their pride and joy. A high school football star, Marine war hero (in their eyes), and the future of Sunrise Ranch. There was no chance of them understanding or approving of my persona: "Mustang" the dark romance reader and masktoker. And they certainly wouldn't approve of me writing things like my current passion project, a dark romance book of my own making.

Laughing to myself, I took a sip from the beer and set it down before opening my laptop, TikTok already popping up on my screen. I clicked the refresh button, and my notifications appeared, more than I had the energy to go through. I did, however, like to respond and "liked" most comments to keep engagement.

It was then that a comment on one of my recent videos caught my eye. The video was filmed in one of the barns on the property, the camera aimed at a small flatbed trailer parked inside. The song "Jekyll and Hyde" by Five Finger Death Punch played and as the music dipped, a body fell from out of the camera's view, landing with a thud that shook the trailer.

A moment later, I dropped down beside it—dressed in a black muscle tee, black denim jeans, and boots with my face painted black beneath my cowboy hat and skull-face mask. The video played on repeat as I focused on not so much the comment itself but the display photo and username of the account. It was a close-up of a pair of beautiful brown eyes, while an elegant and feminine skull mask covered her from the nose down. I screenshotted the display picture and zoomed in on the eyes.

Found you.

Clicking on her username "MorphineKiss," I was brought to her profile and began sifting through it.

"Thirty-three-year-old masktoker, UK... Well, hello."

Over the next few hours, I went through and watched every one of her videos, getting to know her. I knew her favorite book series was the **Vicious Lost Boys** by Nikki St. Crow, and her favorite male main character so far was Vayne, **The Dark One**. I'd read the books already. I would have to make some themed content tomorrow to help bait her attention even more.

Her choice in books and favorite character told me quite a bit about her as well. She likely had a shadow daddy kink that went along with being chased, consensual non-consent, and other triggers and kinks of that nature—perfect.

The only frustrating piece of information I learned going through her profile was that she likely lived in (or very close to) a city called Leeds in the United Kingdom, based on the fact she'd tagged it as her location in at least ten videos.

Adjusting my position on my bed, I shook my head. I would have to teach her to be more careful with how much information she put out there. Deciding to subtly initiate things, I clicked the "follow back" button and shut my laptop, setting it on the fridge and going to sleep.

The next day, I'd woken up to a wave emoji, a compliment on my content, and a "thanks for the follow!" After that, we'd messaged one another consistently throughout the entirety of the day. On the nights she didn't work, she'd stay up late so that I could message her or sneak calls to her between chores on the ranch. Some days, I'd saddle up one of the horses and FaceTime her through the entire ride, promising that one day I'd have her on a horse right beside me—once I taught her how to ride, of course.

Lost in the memories, a shifting in my arms pulled my attention back down to the angel beside me. Her eyes fluttered open before closing again. "James, it is you." Sera smiled.

Chuckling softly, I moved back to the tub and carefully eased her into the warm water. "Yes, it's me, Harps. Let's get you cleaned up."

My arms sank below the surface as I eased her body into the warm, scented water. My hand had barely enough time to reach up and cut off the tap when her eyes shot open again with far more awareness this time. She sat upright, splashing water over the side. And then I was trapped in a very wet and surprisingly strong hug as Sera threatened to pull me into the tub with her as my balance was put off.

"Oh my fates! I can't believe you're here in person! Wait—" Her excitement washed away in what I suspected was a mix of shock, embarrassment, and confusion.

Pulling back, Sera crossed her arms over her breasts, her eyes moving side to side as she took in the room and then locked her eyes on me. Allowing her the moment, I moved back on my knees, adjusting a few times at the discomfort caused by my now-drenched briefs.

"The mask… that was you… James!" she exclaimed, her jaw dropping. But soon after, the smile I'd been staring at through my phone's screen for the better half of a year emerged.

All I could do at that moment was nod my head. "Yeah, princess. Hope I didn't scare you too bad," I said with a smirk.

"You ass! Fuck that! That was hot." Her hand reached out for me once more, and I leaned forward, mimicking the gesture.

With each of us cupping the back of the other's head, our lips crashed together in repeated assaults, my teeth instinctively biting at her bottom lip. The rhythm broke, however, when she pulled back. And before I knew it, my cheek was stinging from a swift slap.

"You scared the shit out of me! What, with the book moving and appearing in the window like that! Could have given me a heart attack." Her face went stern and her not-so-foreign-to-these-ears accent made her sound even more displeased.

I knew her better than that.

"Come now, princess. You can pretend all you want, but you loved every fucking minute of it," I growled out at her, leaning into her ear and taking a soft nip on her lobe before pulling back.

"Fucker…" she murmured as she settled into the water, as if just now realizing she was in the tub.

With that, I pushed to my feet and moved around to sit on the stool behind her. "That's what I thought, princess," I said with a smile as I picked up a cup, filling it with warm bath water.

Then, with my free hand, I reached around and placed a

finger under her chin, ushering her to tilt back. She followed my gesture like a good girl, and I poured warm water over her head. Repeating the gesture till I'd wet every inch of her beautiful obsidian hair. I picked up the bottle of shampoo from beside the tub and squirted some into my hand, beginning to massage and lather it into her scalp. The rich vanilla scent filled the air, and I realized the moment she recognized it because she leaned forward and turned slightly, looking down at the floor to see the bottle.

"Coco & Eve? How did you know that was my favorite shampoo?" she asked, her voice almost suspicious. But not scared.

"Attention to detail. In every teasing photo you'd send me from your bathroom, I noticed the same bottles were always in the shower."

As I rinsed out her hair, I became captivated by the suds running down her delicate neck, over her collarbone, and meeting the water right at the start of her breasts. My cock, lacking any control, hardened instantly but I didn't obey it and wouldn't give in to my own lust. Not yet. Tonight was about pleasing my girl. Lord knew she'd been far over due for a man's touch.

Once the shampoo was rinsed out, I began working the conditioner down her hair.

"James, this is so nice. I didn't expect this. Where did you learn to wash hair?"

I couldn't help but chuckle softly as my fingers moved to the back of her neck. "Washing out the horses' manes and tails on the ranch," I replied truthfully, and the laugh that came from her was the most contagious thing I'd ever heard, and then I was laughing with her.

"Well, I hope I have nicer hair than a horse."

"I reckon just about," I teased her back.

Before she had the chance to respond, though, I pressed

firmly into the sides of her neck with the thumb and trigger finger of my left hand while my right squeezed her shoulder. Her already-fading laughter cut off with a gasp and a moan.

"Fuck…" was all she managed to let out as I pressed harder, intent on working out every inch of this woman's tension. When I felt one shoulder was loosened enough, I switched to the other side while continuing on her neck.

She was leaning back into my hand, arching her spine and rolling her shoulders like she was guiding me to her worst spots. Her breathing was getting heavier, her moans a mix of pain and pleasure, and it was driving me mad.

Continuing to massage with one hand, I leaned forward, reaching the other down into the water and slowly moving it along her large, full breasts. Taking one nipple between my fingers, I pinched and twisted it, enjoying the light gasp of pleasure that escaped her. I then slowly reached across her chest and did the same to her other nipple before gliding my hand farther down her body. From what she'd told me, it had been years since she'd been willingly touched, even longer since a man had touched her right. She was going to learn that only I was capable of touching her properly.

Inching closer on the stool to allow myself better access, I moved my fingers between her legs, slow enough to allow her the opportunity to stop me if she wanted to. She didn't. Her legs parted more for me and my fingertips glided down over her most-private area, my palm cupping her pussy. A moan escaped her lips, and I pressed forward, moving my hand in small up-and-down motions, feeling her heat increase even against the already-warm water.

Lowering my face, I brushed my lips against her neck in soft kisses. My hand once more gliding up over her pussy. But this time, my fingertips parted her, finding her clit. I started moving them in small circles, matching the rhythm of the kisses I placed up her neck. When I reached her ear, I bit down, tugging and sucking it into my mouth. She moaned and pressed against me —*so responsive.*

I continued working her clit with one hand and massaging her breasts with the other till I heard her moaning my name.

"James, don't stop... I'm so close," she cried out as she leaned into me.

Feeling her body tense, I shifted my hand from her breast to her chin and pulled her into a passionate kiss just before her legs began to quake. She came for me, her shaking thighs turning the stillness of the water to a roaring ocean in the midst of a hurricane. Just as quickly as it came on, however, the water calmed as she pried her lips from mine and leaned her head back against me, panting for air.

I kissed her once on her temple with a smile pulling at my face. "Let's get you rinsed out and dried off, Harps."

4

SERA

The amount of care and attention I received from James could almost be considered scary. It was such a drastic change from anything I'd ever had with Micheal that I was in shock.

After James had given me the third most amazing orgasm of my life, all of which occurred in the last few hours, he'd washed out my hair and helped me out of the tub. Leaving me to dry myself off, he stepped out of the bathroom and into the main bedroom that was intended to be for Danielle and me.

I wrapped the towel around myself, then placed my hair up in a towel of its own, pausing when I walked out. The bedroom had been somewhat transformed. The scent of mahogany and sandalwood filled the air, and I spotted at least four candles that had been placed in various corners. The bedding had been straightened out, my book neatly placed on one pillow, mirroring the book I knew James had been reading, *SKIN* by Sybil Knight. Off on the far side of the room, James stood at the window, adjusting the blackout curtains before turning to glance in my direction as the bathroom door shut behind me.

"Well, aren't you a romantic soul, Mr. Mustang?" I said in a flirtatious tone, addressing him by his social media alias while looking him over.

He had changed into a pair of silky black underwear with the United States Marine Corps emblem on them. Apart from that, the man was completely nude, and I could not help but take him in.

James stood at 6'4" with an athletic build, covered in tattoos from his neck to his feet. He kept his hair cut short—very military style—and his beard trimmed. The man looked like a modern day Viking god covered in hair, tattoos, and muscle. His features the perfect blend of Clint Eastwood, Bradley Cooper, and Tom Hardy.

He smirked, and I cursed my lustful body for pulsing for the man again, after he'd already gotten me off three times in one night.

"I figured we could wind down proper, cozy up in bed together, and read our books. I put your bookmark back where it should be, by the way." He chuckled.

"Well, thank you for that. Though I don't think I'll be able to enjoy another masked man scene quite as much now. Not that I'm complaining, of course." I laughed, pulling the covers back on the bed and picking up my book.

James climbed in beside me, doing the same before reaching one arm out to pull me in close. "Good, because I'm not apologizing one bit."

He opened his book, able to comfortably hold it and turn the pages in one of his massive hands. Meanwhile, I made myself at home in his opposite arm, propping my book up above my face. This felt so foreign but natural at the same time.

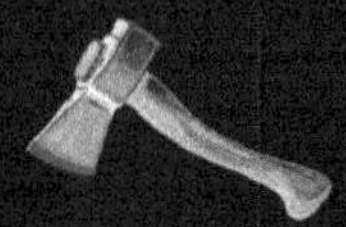

SUNDAY

When I opened my eyes, the sunlight was just barely starting to creep in through the curtains. Rolling over expecting to see James still asleep beside me, I was surprised to find him not only gone but his side of the bed perfectly made as if no one had ever been there. Mildly alarmed, I sat up and looked around the room. There was no physical trace of the man. The only evidence that I hadn't lost my mind was the warm woodland scent of his cologne in the air.

I climbed off the bed, put on some black Gymshark leggings and an oversized black hoodie from my luggage, and left the bedroom in search of my masked man. As I opened the bedroom door, it became apparent where I would find him. The sweet aroma of bacon cooking greeted me as I moved to the steps and down the stairs. Turning into the kitchen, I spotted him standing in front of the stove, wearing faded blue jeans and a white T-shirt that hugged his chest, his tattooed arms the perfect complement.

"Wasn't sure how much longer you'd be sleeping. Figured sunrise was a safe bet," he said, flipping the bacon over piece by piece with a fork. He hadn't even looked over a shoulder, clearly having heard me come down the stairs.

"How long have you been awake?" I said, rubbing the sleep from my eyes as I sat down on one of the kitchen bar stools.

He walked over to the toaster, dropped two slices in, and pushed the lever down. "Little more than an hour I'd expect. I'm used to waking up before the sun—ranch life and all. So I went out and moved my truck up in front of the cabin and figured I'd fix up some breakfast for us."

The toast popped up a moment later and he started serving the food, bringing a plate of eggs, bacon, and toast over to me first. Setting it down in front of me before joining me with his own.

"Well, thank you. That's really sweet of you. So, how long have you been planning all this?" I asked.

He took a few bites, then responded, "Ever since you told the group you'd be getting here early by yourself. It took a little planning, and hiding my truck where you wouldn't see it wasn't the easiest. But, overall, I'm rather pleased with the way it went." Chuckling, he took another bite while slowly looking me over.

I knew he was undressing me with his forest-green eyes, and suddenly my underwear was ruined. The subtleties of this man did me in, everything from his physique to his southern drawl.

"Wait… What are we going to tell the others when they get here?" I could feel my cheeks heating up.

It was obvious to everyone in the group's Discord server that something had developed between me and James. We didn't disclose anything to the group because we didn't realize how immediate our connection would be.

"Don't worry about it. Danielle was in on the entire thing, actually. Had to make sure she didn't decide to come up early, being your best friend and all. Only thing she doesn't know is that she won't be staying in the main bedroom with you." He took a final bite of his food and began cleaning up.

"What do you mean? That was the plan," I said, watching James wash the dishes in the sink, the veins in his tattooed fore-arms seeming to bulge as he scrubbed one of the pans clean.

What was it about strong men in white T-shirts doing chores that was so sexy?

"You're right. That *was* the plan. Plans change, though. I'm staying in the main bedroom with you." He answered my ques-tion, only glancing at me for the briefest of moments.

"But what will Danielle say? What will the others think?" I felt my cheeks heating up for a second time in a matter of minutes.

"I don't give a damn what they feel or think on the matter," he said, pausing his chore and looking over to me with those piercing emerald eyes. "I've waited for this trip for so long. I'm going to spend every night fucking you till you have to stand the entire flight home. We're going to need that large bed for everything I'm going to do to you, Sera." His eyes looked me up and down once more before that dangerous smirk crossed his lips and he returned his focus to the dirty dishes.

He did it again. *How could someone doing an innocent task such as washing dishes, after cooking me a nice simple breakfast, turn around and say something so filthy and so attractive in the same instance?*

Just when I opened my mouth to respond, the front door opened with a *thud* as it hit the inner wall.

"We're here, bitches!" a peppy female voice called out, followed by the unmistakable sounds of luggage bags rolling over and being dropped onto the hardwood floor.

Spinning on my bar stool, I caught sight of Lola, Danielle, and Jade—Brian bringing up the rear with a sheepish look on his face. Lola was standing front and center, and despite what some would call a *gothic* or *heavily-alternative appearance*, she was clearly the source of the overly-cheery announcement.

With the all-black clothing, facial piercings, and tattoos scattered all over her body (including the front of her throat) most would likely be intimidated by Lola at first glance. Find her off-putting. However, this five-foot-six goth bat made a beeline for me, wrapping me in a hug before I was able to do more than stand up from my seat. Soon, the other two girls were joining in, and I was consumed by a massive group hug, the excited voices all blurring together.

"Oh my god, this is amazing!" Lola squealed.

"I can't believe it! You're beautiful!" Danielle chimed in.

"Let's start drinking already!" Jade blurted out, the scent of something cinnamon already on her breath.

5

JAMES

As the ladies attacked Sera, it was hard not to laugh. Even harder not to cover my ears at the high-pitched tones of each of them squealing and trying to talk over one another. Reminding me of the effect you get when you pour the slop in the pigs trough at feeding time. The thought created a funny image in my head—not one I'd ever voice out loud, though.

I moved around the gathering of women, towards Brian with an outstretched hand. Brian stood a bit shorter than I was, just under six feet with crimson hair and an average build. Judging by the look on his face, I could tell the ride up here from the airport with the ladies was likely torture.

"Welcome to America," I said, giving him a firm shake. I glanced over at the girls. They all seemed giddy until I noticed Sera managing to pry herself loose to catch her breath.

"James, good to be here. Though I'm regretting the travel arrangements we'd made. Wouldn't you know my noise-canceling headphones would die on the plane before we even landed. The entire drive up, I just listened to the ladies go on about one book man or another. Not that I mind typically, of course, but I couldn't get a word in edgewise, even if I'd wanted to." He let out a sigh and a soft chuckle, looking like a man who had just been rescued from a bad storm.

"Sounds like you're in need of a beer, my friend." I laughed, clapping him on the shoulder and gesturing to the fridge, where I grabbed us each a Budweiser and popped them open. "To good times," I said, passing him his and tapping our bottles together before taking a long swig.

It was five o'clock somewhere after all.

The sound of the bottles clinking was all it took to break up the chatter.

"James! Hello, handsome, are you going to serve us ladies too?" Lola cried out, peeling off from the group and over to me.

Smiling up at me, she reached around my waist, her body flush with mine as her nails dug into my back. I set my beer down on the counter and gently placed my hands on her forearms, freeing myself from her grip and quickly opening the fridge. Brian's face visibly cringed, but with his back to the group, I was the only one who seemed to notice.

Prior to Sera arriving, I'd stocked not only this fridge but the icebox out on the porch with enough food and drinks to last the entire group for the duration of the stay. The cabin was fully stocked with a mix of beers, liquors, and hard seltzers. I grabbed four White Claws and passed them to Lola, who smiled and snatched them from my hand. After she distributed them to the other girls, each one took their turn coming over to hug and greet me as if suddenly aware of my presence.

After a brief post-trip conversation, Sera went with the girls to show them their rooms, and I escorted Brian to his.

"So, mate, what time did you get in? Surprised you beat us here. Get on with Sera all right so far?" he said, tossing his bags on the bed he'd claimed for himself.

The room featured a full-size bunk bed and a couch off to the side that could be pulled out into a small sleeper. The original idea had been for the three guys to share the largest room, apart from the main bedroom upstairs.

"I got here early last night actually. Stocked the house and made sure everything was good to go," I said, lifting my beer to my lips as I sat on the small couch and leaned into the cushions with my other arm draped across the back.

Brian paused in the middle of unpacking and raised a curious brow at me. "Oh, I see. Well then, you must have been here to greet Sera? Sure she appreciated that. Being in a foreign country, all alone up in the woods." He resumed his unpacking, claiming some of the drawers for himself and stowing away his things.

"Yeah, I reckon she appreciated it well enough," I said, not eager to give him all the details of last night's activities.

He stood in front of the dresser, pulling out another drawer, when something seemed to click in his mind and he began to scan the room. With a fair idea as to what he was looking for, I continued to sit and sip on my beer.

"Mate, where're your things?" he said, his eyes finally landing on me again.

"Oh, they're upstairs, in the main bedroom," I said with an uninterested shrug.

"Well, now, would seem she appreciated you coming here early rather much, hm?" Brian said with a laugh.

I was just about to respond when we heard banging on the stairs before a tall, slender, long-haired man appeared in the doorway.

"Well, the fuck do we have down here? What's up, bro-bitches!" Robert stepped into the room, arms outstretched. He instantly grabbed Brian and slapped him on the back.

I stood and moved in his direction, offering my free hand only to be pulled into a one-armed hug, managing not to spill my beer—thanks to my quick reflexes. "Rob, good to meet you face-to-face. I take it Lyndsey is up with the ladies?"

He nodded and looked from the top bunk to the couch, as if deciding which he wanted. "Yeah, man, she took her shit to her room and went searching for the other girls. She tells me you got up here early to surprise Sera, huh? You dirty dog you. How'd it go? You smash or what, bro? Don't skip on the deets!" He punctuated his words with a light jab to my shoulder, and I allowed it.

"Makes sense you'd have Danielle help with your planning. Take it she didn't originally know she wouldn't be staying with Sera, though?" Brian said from behind Robert with a smirk.

"What? Broooooo, Danielle is going to be pissed at you," Robert added.

I just smirked and shook my head. "Well, Danielle will get over it. I'm sure she won't mind too much. As for last night's events, I'm not one to kiss and tell, but I will say Sera and I are getting along just fine." I paused, my eyes looking from one guy to another. "So, hands off, clear?" My tone dropped deeper than intended but with the proper amount of threat in it. And from their expressions, I knew they understood clear as day.

Brian nodded. I wasn't so much worried about him, though. He'd had a thing for Lola since the conception of the group. He was quiet and sophisticated. And unlike myself and Robert, he was strictly a Booktok guy. All of his content was focused on providing really in-depth reviews and ratings of every book he read. Not just romance or dark romance either, which was something else impressive about the guy. He read anything from character development, to science fiction like *Star Wars*, to dark romance books where the main male characters were ogres or demonic clowns.

His page was actually pretty big for being more tame, around 30k followers in just a few months. To add to his list of accomplishments, he was typically ARC reading for at least three authors at a time and paid to do it in many cases. He was by far my favorite of the guys.

Robert, on the other hand, hit on anyone and everyone, as if his only requirement for a woman was that she had a pulse, and even that was questionable. Apart from that, though, everyone enjoyed him. He was the class clown. Whether it was his comical masked, Deadpool, surfer guy, stoner content *or* his unpredictable comments and memes in the chat, he was easily the life of the party as far as the men went. He'd hit on all the women on this trip but never in a way that had crossed the line.

Either way, if I had to put money on it, I'd say Lyndsey was his focus. When we'd all picked Shingletown as our getaway destination, he'd immediately told Lyndsey he could pick her up since he lived in San Diego and she was in Los Angeles. They didn't seem like they'd be a totally bad match either; though one was certainly more Beverly Hills and the other more beach bum.

Normal conversation resumed, as the guys unpacked their belongings and I got comfortable on the couch and pulled out my phone. Placing one earbud in, I opened the app to the hidden cameras I'd installed all over the cabin before Sera had arrived and began flipping through each of their feeds one at a time. I didn't place a camera in either of the other girls' bedrooms. I was no pervert and had no intention of spying on any of the other women here.

Just when I was about to close the app and return my attention to the guys, however, I heard my name on the feed and paused, curiosity getting the better of me.

6

SERA

"All right, spill the tea about you and James!" Lyndsey demanded, her arms crossed over her chest. She'd arrived not long after the four of us moved into one of the two rooms so that Lola and Danielle could start unpacking, while we got each other all caught up on the gossip.

"He just came up here to make sure I was safe, since I was all alone in a new place. You know him, quite the over-protective big brother type." I laughed nervously, knowing that *I* wouldn't even buy that was all there was to it. All of a sudden, my folded hands in my lap were so interesting that I couldn't be bothered to look up at my friends.

"No point in holding anything back. I know he hit up Danielle forever ago to make sure she wouldn't come up here early with you." Lyndsey smiled and leaned against the wall, and I could feel the blood rushing to my cheeks.

"Oh my god, I fucking knew it, bitch!" Lola's eyes felt like they were burning into me and her tone seemed… resentful almost? "I told you girls!" In the blink of an eye, Lola was sitting beside me on the bed without leaving any space to breathe.

Before I had the opportunity to move, Danielle was on my other side. "You two have been sharing each other's content a lot more! I wasn't surprised when he told me he planned on surprising you," she added, her voice sweet like honey with an American southern drawl that I couldn't deny still did something to me.

It complemented her strawberry-blond hair and brilliant freckles. The sight of her had always made me feel some strange way, and at one point, we'd entertained the idea of being *more*. In the end, we'd established we were best as good friends. But sitting here beside her put other thoughts in my mind. Thoughts I couldn't shake.

Jade dropped down on the bed across from me, White Claw in hand while appearing hesitant to speak but she did anyway. "Actually, Sera, I wasn't going to say anything. It's not really my business at all but…" She paused to look around at the other girls, then seemed to non-verbally add: *since everyone else is.* "He doesn't really share everyone else's stuff nearly as much, and I don't think he's even collabed with any of my videos before, yet he's done so with many of yours. I'm not complaining. Honestly, I think it's cute." She got quieter towards the end, as if she suddenly regretted having said anything at all or maybe she was just afraid she was being rude.

Jade was an inch or so taller than I was with a slightly heavy build, dark hair, the friendliest smile, and the sweetest voice to go along with it. The other girls and I had been telling her that she should get into voice acting or narrating for months now, but she was far too shy. I loved that about her, truthfully. While Danielle was certainly my best girlfriend in the group, Jade was a close second. Though I'd never tell the other girls that. They were all amazing in their own right.

"Well, he's really… sweet and caring and affectionate and strong and—"

I was beginning to trail off when Lola slapped a hand down on my thigh. "Oh my god, you fucked him!"

Lacking any sort of poker face, I could feel my cheeks heating up and bit down on my lower lip.

"I fucking knew it when I went upstairs to check out the main room and found his bags and mask in the closet. You're lucky I love you, Sera, but you better believe I'm using that tub!" Lyndsey said, my eyes widening as my mind trailed back to what he'd done for me in that same tub last night.

"Um, yeah, of course," I managed to let out softly.

Perhaps sensing my discomfort, Danielle turned the focus on Lyndsey. "So how about you and Mr. MaskedSurfer?" She was referring to Robert. "You two have a nice drive up here? Make any stops on the way?" she asked in a teasing tone.

Lyndsey scoffed, pushing herself off the wall to sit beside Jade on the other bed before leaning over. Lowering her voice to ensure only the five of us could hear. "It wasn't horrible, but if I had to listen to him sing one more song or crack one more joke about giving him road head, I was going to throw myself out of the car."

All of our eyes snapped up to meet hers.

Lyndsey shrugged, pushed her purchased double-Ds up in the air, and licked her lips. "Well, it did pass the time, and we are on *holiday* as Sera says, and since she also already has her claws in James…"

The room exploded into laughter, teasing, and questions.

"Erghmm."

Lost in conversation, we hadn't even noticed the towering figure in the doorway. All five of our mouths clamped shut and we looked over in perfect sync. And there, leaning against the doorframe, was James. His arms crossed over the chest of his white V-neck shirt.

"You ladies getting settled in all right?" The smirk on his face was brilliant. Who knew how long he'd been standing there just listening? *How many times could I blush in one day?*

Lyndsey was the first of us to snap out of the shock of being caught mid-gossip as well as the brief daydream I know we were all having while taking in his image. "James, there you are! We were just talking about you. How dare you corrupt our sweet, innocent Sera!"

"I reckon I may have… Got a little something on the corner of your mouth there, by the way," he responded in a teasing tone that hinted at how long he'd been listening to us.

"Ass." Her hand shot up to cover her mouth as she likely did a quick lick of her lips.

He let out a low chuckle as he peeled off the doorframe. "Was just going to let you ladies know I'll be grilling tonight. Brought plenty of stuff up the mountain. Just wanted to make sure no one's got any crazy allergies before I start seasoning and marinating." After a moment, he nodded, taking our silence for his answer. His eyes locked on to me briefly before he stepped away and out of sight. "Right then, as you were, ladies."

"Fuck me, the Texan accent on that man's gravelly voice… Fuck, Sera, you're going to share him, right? Like, we can take turns doing threesomes? They're fun—trust me," Lola said while shamelessly drooling over James.

"Lord Almighty, Lola, ease off. This isn't one of our books," Jade cut in before I could even think of a response.

Later that afternoon, everyone had broken up to do their own thing. Lola and Lyndsey were going live on TikTok in the den area. The two of them together looked like they could have been the real-life Glinda and Elphaba from *Wicked* with their contrasting styles.

Meanwhile, Jade, Danielle, and I were outside at the stone patio area beside the large stream that ran behind the cabin, each with our own book. It was a cozy spot with multiple chairs placed around a large stone firepit.

The boys were all hanging out on the deck just above us, where James was getting ready to fire up the grill, while Brian and Robert offered crucial support from the sidelines as they continued with what must have been their fourth or perhaps sixth beer of the day.

The peaceful sound of the rippling water and the gentle breeze rustling the towering trees above us made for the perfect ambience for reading. The same autumn breeze that also sent a shiver over me.

"Bit chilly…" I said, setting my book down in my lap so that I could take the ends of each sleeve and pull them farther down.

"Isn't it? We need to get a fire going. Is there any firewood?" Danielle stood and made her way over to me before pausing to look towards the cabin. "Hmmm, it would seem we have plenty of firewood. Just need someone for the labor," she said in a mischievous tone.

Turning in my seat to follow her gaze, I spotted a large pile of logs, none of which looked cut up or moveable. "Well, shit…" I said under my breath.

"Oh, don't worry. We just need to use our feminine powers." Danielle giggled, moving my book aside before dropping down into my lap.

I felt my cheeks burn crimson at her sudden closeness. The warm, floral scent of her perfume dancing around me. Instinctively, my right hand moved to rest on the small of her back, just under her sweater.

We exchanged one long, tense look before she broke the silence, peering up at the deck above us and calling out, "Oh, boys, could one of you big strong men come chop some of this wood and help get us a fire going? Pretty please? We're getting cold."

In case her plea wasn't enough encouragement, Danielle wrapped her arms around my head and pulled my face to her chest. She shuddered, really selling our certain demise. What the guys wouldn't be able to see from this angle was how much heat was growing in my core or the claw marks I was undoubtedly making on her back.

7

JAMES

I'd just hooked up the propane tank when I heard Danielle call out from below. Standing up, I lit the grill as I turned and looked to Brian and Robert.

"One of you boys got that?" I said, raising a brow to them. I certainly didn't trust either of them to grill, one being not only a city boy but British and the other being a Californian.

"Bruh, you know what? I could totally do that, but I tweaked my shoulder the other day falling off my board and just shouldn't aggravate it," Robert said while slowly rotating one shoulder as if trying to work out a bad kink.

"Right then, suppose it just leaves me then now, doesn't it?" Brian said with a nervous chuckle. "There a chainsaw or something around to use?"

It took every ounce of my restraint to not facepalm as I looked over at him and watched as he slowly started to inch towards the stairs that led to the patio area below us.

"Christ…" I said under my breath, turning my Chevrolet ball cap around backwards. "You both get the burgers going, do the asparagus too, but don't touch the kabobs. I'll fix those up when

I'm done." I slapped Brian on the shoulder, who seemed to deflate under my touch at the thought of not having to do the physical labor.

"Right on, man, easy stuff. Don't worry. We got it," Rob said, moving over to the grill, beer in hand, suddenly forgetting about his pained shoulder.

I stopped at the top of the stairs, my eyes locking on to Danielle grinding back and forth on Sera's lap. A fire started to build in my chest but I let out a slow exhale, reducing it to a small ember.

Reaching the base of the stairs, I headed in their direction. A quick blur of motion in the distance told me Jade was now awkwardly looking away. Pausing behind Sera, I threw a challenging glance at Danielle before following it with a teasing raise of an eyebrow.

Then I leaned forward and took Sera's chin between my finger and thumb and guided her gaze up to meet mine. "Cold, Harps?"

Out of my peripherals, I could see Danielle's mischievous grin. There was no need to guess her intentions; Sera had certainly discussed her fantasy of having the three of us spend an evening together. Not that I was particularly thrilled with the idea of anyone else playing with my things.

But I would endure.

"Yeah, a bit," Sera said softly under her breath, her eyes meeting mine.

"No worries. I'll get you ladies a fire going. Later, I'll warm you up myself." I leaned down farther and pressed my lips to hers.

"Oh Lord, get a room. Danielle doesn't want you two fucking with her right there," Jade said from the sidelines.

Biting onto Sera's bottom lip, I tugged it softly as I stood upright. My eyes having caught the way Danielle's cheeks flushed beyond the chill. Then I stepped back and made my way over to the logs.

I sat one log on top of the other and grabbed the nearby axe, weighing it in my hand before glancing over to the women. I refocused on the task, raising the axe up and bringing it down with a crack, splitting the top log in two. I continued the process, picking up the halves and splitting them once more, letting out a deep huff with each swing.

By my fourth or fifth swing, I heard a gasp from the direction of the patio and looked up to see all three of the women had stopped reading their books and were staring at me. Just as my eyes landed on them, they all snapped their attention back to their books, Danielle still seated on Sera's lap.

I shook my head and resumed my work. It didn't take long before I was bringing the axe down for the last time, leaving the edge of the blade stuck in the base log and releasing the handle. Lifting the lower portion of my shirt, I wiped the sweat from my face. Then, a bundle in one arm and another in my opposite hand, I walked over to the firepit and started stacking them up with some dried leaves and twigs in the center.

"So, James, do you have a cute younger brother or anything? Or even a sister maybe?" Jade asked as I struck a match and lit the kindling.

"Two little sisters, and before you ask, the answer is *no*. I don't have any hot single friends either. Most of my buddies are either hitched down or scattered across the country." Once the fire was going well enough, I dropped some more of the wood beside the firepit so the ladies wouldn't have to go far to get them and then went back upstairs to the grill. To my relief—and surprise—the guys hadn't burned anything.

Another hour later and the party was in full swing. Everyone gathered around the firepit. Eating, drinking, and joking. Robert played his acoustic guitar off to one side. A mix of popular pop hits that I mostly didn't care for but the energy was good. Lyndsey, Jade, and Danielle all sat near him, listening to the music, while it appeared as though Brian was attempting to shoot his shot with Lola, who was toying with him like a cat with a mouse.

"Bless his heart," I said softly.

"What?" Sera asked from where she was seated on my lap, my left hand resting on her side while my other held my beer.

"Brian. Kid is fawning over Lola something fierce. Poor boy doesn't stand a chance. That girl would chew him up and spit him out if she wanted to." I shook my head and took a sip of my beer, then looked up at Sera. She was dressed in black sweatpants and one of the hoodies from my merch line. My hoodie.

"Yeah, she's really not into him, sadly. Believe she's more into you, to be honest," Sera said, leaning closer to my chest.

"You don't have anything to worry about there, Harps. I like Lola but I've dated her type before—reckless and self-destructive." I shook my head. "I'm a one-woman man. You are all I need, all I desire." My hand squeezed her side, and without setting down my beer, I pulled the serape I'd draped over the arm of the chair across her lap, taking a final sip of my Budweiser before setting the bottle on the ground. My hand slipped under the blanket and between Sera's legs, my fingers pushing against the insides of her thighs.

"James, we can't," she whispered but opened her legs for me anyway.

My hand slowly moved up and pulled the string of her sweatpants, undoing them so that my fingers could easily slip beneath the waistband. I straightened in the seat and raised my lips to her neck just below her ear.

"Be my good girl, and let's see how much control you have," I said as my fingertips glided over her warm pussy, already slick with desire. "Oh, baby, you're so wet for me." I rested my palm over her before slowly moving it back up, parting her with my fingers and resting them gently over her clit. Her body bucked against me as I found her most sensitive spot.

"James, they'll know…" she whispered again as I watched her eyes flick from one person to the next.

"Poker face, baby," I said, as I started massaging her clit.

She gasped, and her body tensed under the hand I was using to brace her. She quickly raised her White Claw to her lips to hide behind it.

"Shh, they'll hear you," I teased as I moved my hand in a quick, small, circular motion. I could feel her desire increase, coating my fingers and beginning to soak the black fabric of her sweatpants. "You're such a horny girl, so eager to come, just craving my touch, aren't you?" I kissed her neck, giving it a soft bite, releasing an exhale of warmth against her skin as I did.

I picked up the rhythm, playing her like an instrument, impressed with how quiet she was, while at the same time feeling challenged. Eager to test her and make her come all over my hand, I changed tack. Already sensing that she was on the verge of an orgasm, likely due to the voyeurism which I knew to be one of her kinks, I decided to make this quick. Slipping my fingers between the apex of her thighs and hooking them, I began pulling and pushing, penetrating her as my palm rubbed at her clit. Her free hand closed around my wrist and her nails sank into my skin, the sweet sting only encouraging me further.

The party continued around us, but Jade glanced our way, her face instantly turning the darkest shade of red, before she looked back to Robert playing the guitar. I kept up the relentless pace until Sera's body tensed again, and I heard the sound of an aluminum can being crushed when her palm clamped around her White Claw. Her pussy gripped at my fingers as if trying to keep them as she trembled.

"That's my good girl," I praised, as I slowly slipped my fingers free and placed them in my mouth. Tasting her. My girl was sweeter than honey, and it took all of my self-control to not carry her upstairs right now and harvest her passion straight from the source.

Overall, the gathering was a picture-perfect scene with good food, good drinks, a warm fire, and the twinkling night sky above. Lyndsey and Lola made themselves cozy by the fire, where Robert began repeating his repertoire of songs on the guitar—*all three of them that we'd heard a handful of times already.* Meanwhile, Brian sat closer to Sera and me, looking like a scared pup unable to come out of his cage.

"Brother, you aren't going to make any progress climbing that mountain if all you do is sit here and stare at the peaks," I said, looking over and passing him a fresh Budweiser from the cooler at my side.

"Aye, I know. She's just so far out of my league. Plus, I don't think she fancies me much. Not like that at least," he said, peering down at the beer in his lap before taking a small sip.

"What she doesn't *fancy* is the lack of confidence. When you're breaking a stallion, it's all about confidence. A woman is the same, maybe more difficult, I reckon." I chuckled and took a drink just as Sera elbowed my chest, causing me to spit a bit out onto my shirt. The three of us broke out into good-hearted laughter until my eyes locked on to something across the patio.

Lyndsey and Lola were sitting on the large stone wall of the firepit, both staring into Lola's phone, undoubtedly laughing at a TikTok video. But what caught my eye was Robert, who was seated on Lyndsey's opposite side, one hand poised near her red Solo cup as he slipped something inside it. Then, concealing the bag in his palm, he stood with guitar in hand and went over to where his case was resting and began putting it away.

Immediately realizing what he had done, I could sense my entire body tense as I nudged Sera. "Let me up a minute, Harps."

"Oh, okay," she said, a bit of confusion in her voice. But she didn't question me, claiming my spot on the chair once I was up.

My mind was racing, my instincts telling me to yell out across the patio for Lyndsey not to drink from her cup, and then break Robert's neck. That, however, could ruin the entire vacation for everyone.

No, I could do this without raising the alarm too much. The Marine Corps and ranch life had taught me to be much more tactful than that.

Taking slightly longer than usual strides, I closed the distance between Lyndsey and myself without looking suspicious. I plastered a grin on my face as I passed her, spun around, and backed into a seated position on her free side, where her drink sat.

"What are you ladies laughing at?" My ass met with her cup, pushing it back into the firepit and spilling the contents.

"James! Fuck, my drink!" Lyndsey cried out just as I sat down, the sound of the ice tumbling out catching her attention.

"Ah, shit, I'm sorry!" I said apologetically, though my eyes were honed in on Robert standing directly across from me. His eyes met mine, and I *knew* he *knew* I *knew*. "I'll go make you another drink." I pushed to my feet and offered Lyndsey a smile before turning to Robert. "Why don't you come with me, brother. Forgot I had something I wanted to show you." I kept my tone level but insistent.

"Yeah, sure thing, man," he answered as I stepped off, leading the way, with Rob tailing behind me.

I opened the sliding glass door to the dining room, allowing him to walk inside first.

"Hey, man, so what's up? You're acting weird, dude," he started to say, turning around just as I shut the glass door behind us.

Before he had the chance to fully face me, my right fist caught him across the jaw, adding momentum and causing his entire body to spin all the way to the floor.

Was it a cheap shot? Maybe, but at this point, I didn't owe the bastard anything.

He landed on his chest, and I kicked him in the ribs until he rolled over onto his back, allowing me to place my size-thirteen Stetson on his throat. Robert squirmed, moving to grab my boot and push it off. But I was a lot stronger than he was and pressed down harder till I felt the change in pressure I knew all too well.

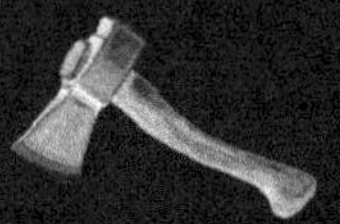

Marjah, Helmand Province, Afghanistan
    13 February 2010

The 3rd Battalion 6th Marines was part of a massive operation to retake the city from the Taliban forces. My company was inserted in the first wave of helicopters in the northern part. The sun hadn't even come up and yet thousands of Marines alongside British and Canadian forces were converging on all sides from the ground and air. Building by building, street by street.

That was the first time I killed a man. My squad had cleared multiple buildings already. I'd fired plenty of shots but it was anyone's guess who'd hit the targets.

We were currently stacked outside another door. Lance Corporal Salinas was the first to enter and cross the room. Private Johnson was the second. As infantry Marines, we'd trained constantly. Practiced how to clear rooms, enter danger zones, and breach a building.

Rule number one: If the first man crosses straight, the second man is meant to button hook, U-turning into the room to clear the corner opposite the Marine before him.

Rule number two: Once the squad starts pouring in, you don't stop; you get in fast and hard.

Johnson forgot rule number one. If he hadn't, he likely would have spotted the hostile hiding in the corner behind the dresser. He didn't and caught multiple 7.62 rounds to the back, dropping instantly.

As the third man, I saw Johnson—aka Scarecrow—go the wrong way. And out of my peripherals, I watched him start to go down. Everything seemed to blur in that moment. I didn't even remember hearing the sound of the AK-47 going off. I just remembered turning the corner and spotting a man with a rifle in his hands. And I remembered pressing the trigger once, maybe twice, but that was all.

A second later, it seemed I was straddling a stranger on the ground, his blood soaking through the trousers of my uniform from multiple holes in his chest. He wasn't dead, though. His eyes looked up into mine. Wide and afraid and glossy. That was when I realized my hands were wrapped around his throat, the full weight of my body pressing down on my arms. On his neck.

I think I heard screaming from behind me, someone yelling for a corpsman and maybe calling out "Samuel," Johnson's first name. I pressed harder on the man's throat and felt a pop and snap, and suddenly he went limp. And then a hand appeared on my shoulder, shaking me.

"Mustang! James!"

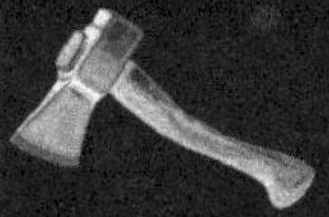

"James! What the fuck, mate!" a male voice yelled, a pair of hands pulling me back by the shoulders. Off Robert and not the stranger in my mind.

I spun on my boots, cocking an arm. Only to stop when my eyes settled on the light-skinned, ginger-haired figure of Brian, his eyes wide with fear and confusion. The sound of hard coughing and wheezing had me looking down and shoving Brian's hands away. Creating some distance as I slammed my boot on Robert's flat hand on the floor when he tried to push himself upright.

"James!" Brian yelled again as Robert cried out in pain.

I held up a hand to silence them. "Bastard tried drugging Lyndsey just now. Poured something into her cup. Luckily, I saw it before she had the chance to drink it."

Brian paused and looked at me, then down at Robert. "Fucking hell, that's why you knocked her drink over. Knew you weren't snookered."

I nodded and returned my attention to Robert. Stepping in front of him, I grabbed him by the collar and landed one more right hook. Sending a tooth flying across the floor this time. "I'm not going to let you ruin this trip for the girls, so I'm not going to kill you and I'm not going to tell them what a fucking piece of shit you are... yet. You are going to get up, grab your shit from the room, jump in your car, and get the fuck out of here. Now. Am I clear?" I said, allowing my spit to splatter over his face.

He shook his head slowly, and I could tell from the way his eyes were moving that he was disoriented. "My... my guitar," he muttered, blood trickling down from where his tooth had been.

"You had a family emergency and forgot to grab it. You aren't going anywhere near those women. That's my guitar now." Standing, I looked to Brian and then towards the closed sliding glass door that was vibrating from the music playing outside. Chances were the girls didn't hear anything. "Brian, go back out there. Bring Lyndsey a Long Island. If they ask about me or Robert, say we are having a guy chat."

Brian nodded, glancing at Rob's bloodied face, then stumbled over to the kitchen, where he made Lyndsey's drink before heading back outside.

"Let's go, asshole," I said as I dragged Robert to his feet and shoved him towards the bedroom to grab his things. I was going to make sure he left.

8

ROBERT

"**S**tupid fucking hick-ass cowboy. Fucking cockblock is what he is. Bitch-ass Texan. Fuck him!" I cursed under my breath, having realized James was nowhere in sight.

The man had been hounding me like Uncle Sam, not letting me even so much as take a piss or wash the blood from my face. He'd shoved me all the way down the hall to grab my belongings. Rushing me.

He'd given me thirty seconds. Then anything not in my bag stayed. When I'd argued, he'd pressed a freakishly large knife against my throat, like the one Rambo had. James never talked about what he did in the military, but I didn't doubt he'd killed before and would again if I pushed my luck.

Staggering up to my car, I looked around for James but he was nowhere in sight. My hand reached for the button that would open the trunk and froze halfway. "I should go back there. Round the house and tell the ladies James went mad. Accuse him of telling me to stay away from Lyndsey, claim that he wanted her and Sera to himself," I grumbled.

Then the chill of the mountain air hit my incredibly sensitive bleeding gums and busted face. With that thought, I opened the trunk and tossed my backpack inside before unzipping it to make sure I had my drugs. I grabbed an edible and popped it into my mouth.

Feeling defeated, I moved around, dropped into the driver's seat, and slammed the door shut. "Wouldn't even let me grab my guitar. What does he care if I fuck Lyndsey…? Bastard is fucking that British whore anyway."

I placed my phone in its holder and started up the car. Then, seeking to improve my headspace, I reached into the center console and pulled out a baggie. One short dip of my little pocket knife and two snorts later and I was already feeling better. After a quick burnout, I was driving away from the cabin.

Fuck them.

Taking a hit of my weed pen and leaning forward, I attempted to navigate the dark country road. "Siri, play music," I said out loud and was answered with "Hotel California" by the Eagles.

"Such a lovely face, plenty of room at the Hotel California, any time of year."

Just as I began to sing along with the chorus and settle into the seat, I felt something hit my side. Hard. Followed by a rush of warmth and wetness. Then a sharp, burning sensation.

"What the fuck!" I screamed, reaching a shaky hand to my side where a pair of knuckles was wrapped around what I knew was a knife.

Fear gripped me, and in a panicked state, I slammed my foot down on the gas pedal instead of the brakes. My body jolted hard as the car jetted forward. With a loud rattling *thud*, it seemed to jump when the tire hit something.

As the vehicle settled back down, the wheel jerked to the right and all momentum came to a sudden stop with a thunderous crash. My neck snapped forward and my face collided with the steering wheel. I must have blacked out, because the next thing I knew, the car was shaking, my forehead still resting on the steering wheel. My body was throbbing, as if a really wild wave had just knocked me off my board and threw me into a rock bed.

"And that is why you should always wear your seat belt, Robert," I heard a muffled, strange, almost polite-sounding voice call out from in front of me.

Unaware of my own decision to do so, I felt my head slowly and painfully rise. My vision was blurred by liquid that was likely my blood.

"James?" I managed to cough out as I desperately attempted to rub the blood from my eyes.

The figure remained cloudy as it crouched low on the hood of my car, the tree I clearly hit behind him. "You should have stayed away from my girl," he said as he leaned through the hole where my windshield once was.

Suddenly, a tugging at my side broke my attention from the figure. I looked down and watched in horror as he pulled a massive knife out of my torso. My body trembled when he tapped me on the nose with the tip and chuckled. That was when my vision focused enough to make out the familiar mask looking back at me with deep, dark sockets for eyes. Half a black skull and a single screw coming out of the forehead. And half a slick, indistinguishable face, apart from one red slash.

Mustang.

"James! What, man? I never touched Sera. I'm leaving! I'm sorry. Please don't kill me." My senses were in full panic mode, the chemical cocktail of cocaine, weed, and alcohol being falcon-punched into overdrive. Adding to the list of unfortunate circumstances was the fact I was bleeding all down my face and had begun to effectively waterboard myself.

"Mustang, please," I cried—though I was unsure if I made any noise beneath the weight of terror pressing on my lungs. I reached up and again tried to rub the blood from my eyes.

"Hush, Robert, I'm going to give you a chance to live. I believe you're sorry and I am a gentleman after all," Mustang cooed from beneath his mask.

The sound of shifting shattered glass hit my ears, each painful note making my skin crawl. Then his hands were brushing my fingers away from my face.

"Oh, my friend, you have something in your eyes. Here, allow me to assist you." His voice came out slow and clipped as he took my head in his large palms.

I opened my mouth to plead with him for mercy, but before I could utter a word, something sharp and hard was being ground into my face. What I felt next was the kind of pain I thought only Hollywood could make up. My eyeballs fucking popped like those giant pimples you saw on Snapchat. I couldn't fucking see it, but I felt that cream cheese-looking pus hit my cheeks, and I screamed.

My hand shot up in disbelief. I couldn't bring myself to actually touch my face, as though I could pretend this wasn't happening for a while longer. The car shook, and the sound of creaking metal told me Mustang had just gotten off the hood. My self-preservation kicked in and my fingers frantically flailed for the door handle. It took a toss of my shoulder, but the door opened, allowing me to stumble out into the wilderness.

I didn't get far before I felt my face gripped between two large gloved hands, accompanied by the softest of whispers. "If you can make it back to the main road, perhaps you will be able to find a way to the hospital. Do that and you get to live. Good luck, Robert."

The moment he released me, I ran. I couldn't see a fucking thing. But I knew, based on the direction I'd gotten out of my car, that I just needed to go straight. Keeping one hand pressed on my side where the bastard had stuck me and the other out ahead, I sprinted forward.

"Oh, do watch for bears!" the asshole yelled after me.

Then I heard the distinct sound of a foot kicking off against hard dirt, and my body froze in panic. Someone was hauling ass down a dirt road.

Down a dirt road. As in, away from me.

I stood motionless till the only thing I could hear was the creaking and ticking of my car turned roadside decor. Once I was certain he was gone, I slowly stumbled in the direction I'd hoped would lead me to a main road, preferably before I bled out.

"Fucking cowboy."

9

SERA

When I caught sight of Brian making his way down the stairs from the deck, *alone*, I felt a twinge of concern and stood from my seat, which I'd moved closer to the fire.

"Where are James and Robert?" I asked, looking behind him while expecting the pair to come back down.

"Oh, um, they're just having a chat. Certainly, they'll be along soon," he responded, avoiding eye contact and almost tripping at the last stair, spilling some of the drink over the edge of the red Solo cup. He continued past me and Jade, over to the other three girls, and handed Lyndsey the cup.

"About damn time! Fuck, I already opened up a White Claw —oh well. Thank god I have two hands!" she yelled out, raising both drinks in the air as "A Bar Song" by Shaboozey played over the boombox.

Suddenly, all of us girls were up and dancing to the music, Danielle grabbing me and taking the lead in what the Americans called two-stepping. I smiled at the sight of Lola dancing with Brian, surprisingly, as Lyndsey and Jade spun around on the stone patio.

A few songs later, James seemed to just appear. He picked up Lola's phone, typed something into it, and the music changed to "Spin You Around" by Morgan Wallen. Then he walked over and tapped Danielle's shoulder, cutting in. Next thing I knew, he was leading me around the impromptu dance floor.

I'd never danced with a man before. Even at my own wedding, my ex-husband had been too drunk by the time our song came on, so I'd danced with my mother instead.

Dancing with James was strangely comforting as he held my body close to his, one hand caressing my hip and the other clasping my hand. I could feel the rough calluses on his palm against mine, strong and rugged yet somehow soft at the same time. After staring intently into his forest-green eyes, I noticed something and my brows furrowed with concern. His knuckles looked swollen and bruised. I glided my thumb over them carefully as I returned my gaze to his.

"What happened?" I asked.

"Nothing at all, princess." He smiled and shook his head before turning me into a spin and pulling me back, placing his lips against mine. I couldn't help but suspect he was trying to shut me up. But at the same time, it worked. "Let's get on out of here," he said with a smile as his lips pulled back from mine and all I could do was nod as I struggled to remember how to breathe. "Night, *errbody*," he said, giving everyone else a wave as he took my hand and led me up the stairs to the deck.

"Use a condom, bitch!" Lola yelled from below.

"Fuck no! Make some pretty babies!" Lyndsey countered even louder.

"Oh my god, ignore them. Goodnight you two! Remember, tomorrow is content day!" Danielle added just as the glass sliding door closed behind us.

The tiniest whiff of bleach hit my nostrils, and I couldn't help but wonder about the source. But as James and I reached the stairs, my mind quickly shifted away from the thought. He guided me to the bedroom, opened the door, and moved to the side.

I slowly stepped forward, my mouth dropping. The room was illuminated by multiple candles while "Eyes on Fire" by Blue Foundation played softly from a speaker on the nightstand. Then my eyes drifted to the perfectly-made bed, where red rose petals were elegantly spread out across the top.

"James, this is beautiful," I said, taking a few more steps towards the bed before turning to face him. Only to find him right in front of me, which forced me to tilt my head back to look up at him.

"No, *you* are beautiful. Nothing else can compare." He spoke softly as one large hand came up to cup my cheek and his lips moved down to meet mine. Our mouths remained still for a moment before he pulled back. "Undress and lie on your stomach. I'm going to give you a massage," he told me.

I looked at the bed, then back at James. "Oh, really, you don't have to. That's sweet, though. You don't want to just take me?" I half smiled, unsure of what to make of all… *this*.

For so many years, the only physical contact I'd had with a man was if I was being bent over and fucked or smacked around. Tonight's dance was already a shocking *first* for me. A man giving me a massage in the same evening might have sent me into shock.

I did as he told me and slowly removed my clothing, my eyes only breaking contact with him when I pulled my top off and dropped it to the floor at our feet. His stare was all-consuming and powerful, the energy between us so electric it could run a small city.

"Here," he said as he pulled something black and silky from his pocket before sliding it over my eyes. His hands took mine and then he was guiding me to the bed, where I lowered myself onto my stomach.

Without my vision, I focused more on my other senses. The

soft bedding beneath me, the soothing music coming from the speaker, and the mixed scents of vanilla and mahogany in the air from the candles. It was so soothing I could have fallen asleep easily.

The floor creaked as James walked around to one side of the bed, and I turned my head to face him, despite not being able to see him. A warm, wet sensation came over my shoulders. And though it was soothing, I flinched at the unexpectedness of it.

"It's okay. It's a special candle made specifically for this. Just relax. Give me control, baby girl."

I heard what I assumed was the candle being set back down on the nightstand as I felt James's palm on one shoulder and then the other. As large and strong as his hands were, they had a remarkable gentleness to them as he started rubbing the massage oil all over my shoulders and neck, applying the slightest bit of pressure as he went. My body melted, every muscle I didn't even know I had relaxing under his touch. He seemed to know exactly where every knot was as he went from one to the next, working them out, causing me to occasionally wince from the brief pain.

He spent his time working every inch of my back from top to bottom, frequently reapplying the heated oil. "Arms up and out to the side," he ordered in a calm tone, and I complied.

His palms closed around my left bicep and he started stroking it, moving one hand over the other as if he was trying to shift all the tension down my arm and out through my fingertips. The pressure and rhythm were so hypnotic I almost didn't notice when he tightened something soft and fur-lined around my wrist, until I instinctively tried pulling my arm back down to my side and couldn't.

"James?" I said in a sleepy voice.

"I've got you, baby girl," he replied just above a whisper. Then he moved around the bed and repeated the action with my other arm and my legs, binding my ankles.

Wiggling each of my limbs, I tested my range of motion to find that none of the restraints were very restricting. The bed shifted, and I assumed he'd climbed on with me while the sound of metal on metal confirmed it.

"Ass up in the air for me, Harps."

Again, I obeyed his command, my core heating up with excitement and curiosity. I felt his hand on the inside of my left thigh and let him guide my legs farther apart. Something clamped down just above the bend of one knee and then the other. Again testing the new sensation, I attempted to move my legs closer together, only to find something hard between them.

"It's a spreader bar, to keep you nice and open for me."

I felt him get off the bed and heard the sound of straps being cinched down as he pulled the wrist bindings tighter to the bedhead and then did the same with my legs.

"If only you could see how beautiful you look for me right now, Harps," he said from somewhere in the room. He was moving around a lot quieter now. I hadn't heard his footsteps on the floor since he started cinching down the restraints. "Is this making you wet? I can see your pussy glistening and I haven't even touched you yet. What a dirty girl you are."

His words had my pussy clenching in response as what felt like multiple strips of leather ran up the inside of my outstretched arm, then reappeared, moving down the center of my back and down over my ass.

"The safe word is red. Do you understand?" he asked.

"Yes, Sir," I replied just before I felt the leather slide up the center of my ass, lightly brushing my wet pussy. Then, for a split second, it was gone, returning with a snap on my ass cheek. "Fuck."

The sting made me cry out, but there was pleasure mixed with the pain. A tingling sensation that came after the shock. With a louder snap, the whip hit my other cheek. Once, twice, and then moved back to the original side. Each crack of the whip forced another moan and cry from me, louder than the one before it, as James increased the force.

"Do you like that, Harps?" He brushed the ends of the whip over my sore ass and then he was gone again.

"Yes," I cried out in a soft whimper, wiggling my hips, wishing he'd touch me, my arousal running down the insides of my thighs.

"Yes?" I heard the urgency in his tone.

"Yes, Sir, I love it. Please whip me harder, Sir." I could not believe the words coming out of my mouth. Being whipped was not something you should enjoy.

But, damn it, then why did it feel so good?

"That's my good girl," he said, before the whip came down even harder across my ass. Multiple times. "What do you say?"

"Thank you, Sir," I responded.

"That's right. In fact, you're being so good I have something for you."

I'd lost track of where he was in the room until a vibrating sound traveled to my right.

"We're going to see how long it takes you to come for me, baby girl," he said as he rubbed something smooth up and down my pussy while taking one of my breasts in his hand, pinching my nipple between his fingers.

Settling it over my clit, he adjusted the intensity and pattern to one he liked and held the device there. The answer to his question was clearly: *not long at all.* In what seemed like seconds, I felt the buildup and rapid release as I orgasmed against the vibrator, my body convulsing as I let out a moan I was certain everyone could hear outside.

10

The sight of her body shaking as she got off on the vibrator had my cock about to break through the zipper of my Levi's. I needed to fuck her, to feel her pussy tight and wet around my cock. I switched the vibrator to its lowest setting and slowly moved it up and down over her pussy. Almost lovingly.

With my free hand, I took my belt and ripped it out of the loops, keeping it in my grip as I shimmied my pants and briefs down my legs. Then I set the vibrator off to the side and positioned myself behind Sera on the bed. Leaning down, I kissed her ass, biting into the flesh before moving lower. I brushed my mouth over her pussy, my face and beard covered with her arousal.

Licking my lips, I released a feral groan. "Fuck, you taste sweeter than honey, baby." I buried my face in her so that I could lap up her arousal. Craving her. "Fuck…" I said with a rumble, my lips not leaving hers, knowing I'd happily die right here in this moment.

I stood to my full height, pulled my shirt off over my head, and threw it to the side before wrapping my belt low around her waist. I then fed the end through the buckle, looping it twice to make a nice handle. I gripped it firmly in my left fist as my right palm reached down and grabbed my hardened cock. Running the tip between the apex of her thighs while coating it in her arousal.

"I hope you're ready for this, baby girl," I told her as I pressed myself inside her. Slow at first. Savoring the feel of her taking me inch by inch, her body opening for me, swallowing me all the way to the hilt.

We moaned in unison as I sank into her and then began a steady rhythm of sliding a few inches back and forth, feeling her dripping all over my cock.

Such a messy girl.

Pulling back to the tip and gripping the belt buckle handle tighter, I tugged hard, thrusting myself forward into her at the same time. Our bodies collided with a *smack.*

"Fuck, James!" Sera cried out, and I did it again. The headboard creaked as she yanked against the restraints. I raised my free hand and spanked her hard across her already-bruising ass, making her cry out in a mix of pain and pleasure. "Harder please, Sir!"

I built a fast rhythm of pulling her back into me as I thrust into her over and over, my balls growing sore from slapping against her pussy and her arousal coating the insides of my thighs.

"You're going to come for me again, Sera. I want to feel you come on my cock." I continued thrusting into her, picking up the vibrator with my free hand and leaning over slightly to reach around her. Turning it on, I held the vibrator by the end so that I could rest the tip on her clit. I could feel it vibrating against my cock as I fucked her.

And, damn it, it felt so good.

"Oh my God!" she cried out, her pussy tightening around me, her body on the verge of another orgasm.

"No, not God. Pray to me, baby!" I growled out.

Her entire body tensed, then shook against mine as sounds of pure pleasure escaped her lips. Her pussy clenched around my cock, as if commanding it to let loose, and I did.

"Fuck," I groaned as I came hard, thrusting one last time and pulling Sera tight against me, shooting my seed deep into her. She wiggled her hips in small circles, enticing my orgasm all the way through me, the sensation making me shudder.

Once we both stopped shaking, I slowly pulled out of her and removed my belt from around her waist, seeing that it left an imprint and would likely bruise for a while. Next, I undid her restraints and removed her blindfold before falling down beside her on the bed. Both of us were glistening with sweat. Her eyes shut as she attempted to catch her breath. When she opened them, they instantly met mine and we lay there smiling at each other.

I was the first to close the distance, kissing her softly on the forehead and then pressing my lips to hers.

"That was amazing. Definitely a few more firsts for me." She laughed and kissed me back.

"Alexa, turn off," I commanded the Echo Dot, and the device stopped playing the passion-inspired country playlist I'd put together specifically for my time with Sera. I chuckled to myself as a thought popped into my head.

"What's so funny?" she asked, rolling onto her side to face me.

"Oh, nothing, just randomly remembered how when I was a teenager, we would have to burn mixed CDs for occasions like this. Now we can make a playlist on our phones and just send the signal to any device we want, which makes me feel like I'm getting old." I shook my head, looked up to the ceiling, and took a long breath. Trying to calm my heart rate.

"Calm down, grandad. You are hardly a year older than I

am." Sera laughed again while playfully shoving at my shoulder.

"Hm, I suppose so." I laughed with her and gave her a quick kiss before getting out of bed and double-checking the locks on the door and window.

Then I headed to the bathroom, taking my phone with me, and flipped through the security cameras, seeing that at least two of the girls and Brian were still outside. Switching to the inside cameras, I caught the briefest glimpse of a shadow stepping into one of the girls rooms but couldn't tell who it was. I was about to rewind the footage and get a better look when I heard Sera knock on the door before opening it.

"Hey, handsome, I've got to pee."

I quickly closed the app, set the phone on the bathroom counter, and flushed the toilet, then stepped over to wash my hands. "All yours, baby girl. See you in bed."

When I was done, I took my phone with me, plugged it up on the charger, and got in bed. Waiting for my girl to join me.

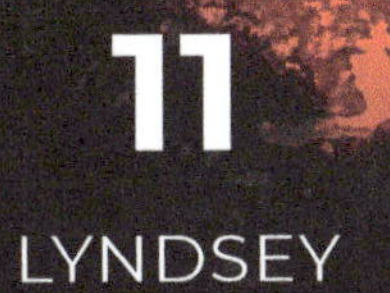

11

LYNDSEY

"Lyndsey, what do you think? Ryat Archer, Leon, Tyson Crawford, or Vayne? Who's the best MMC?" Lola said, looking from Brian to me.

Fuck, she was asking about my favorite main male character.

I knew Ryat Archer and Tyson were from one of the L.O.R.D.S. books, but I had no idea which one. Raising my drink to my lips to buy myself more time, I tried for the life of me to remember where I'd heard the other two names. I had no guess on Leon, and wasn't Vayne that *Batman* villain Tom Hardy played? He was definitely hot as fuck.

"Oh, easy. Vayne, hands down," I said, smiling and picking up my phone as it chimed. "He could break my back any day!"

Lola opened her mouth to respond, but then she and Brian shared a puzzled look, and I couldn't help feeling like I'd gotten something wrong.

"Oh, but you know me, girl. My true love is Zade from *Haunting Adeline.*"

Lola's face wrinkled with confusion. That was a girl who'd never discovered the miracle of Botox—*hopeless.*

I let out a forced laugh, then looked down at my phone again. "MaskedSurfer" appeared in a Discord message notification. My brow furrowed.

At least I think it did.

Having gotten my injections done just a day or two before traveling up here, my face wasn't totally responsive yet, but fuck was I pretty.

I glanced back up to Lola and Brian, but they'd already continued on with their own conversation.

Thank God.

The truth was, I'd never read a complete romance or dark romance book in my life. I owned plenty, at least three bookshelves' worth. I'd buy every single title recommended on Booktok. I'd tried becoming a fitness influencer, a food influencer, even a makeup influencer and never really took off like I know I deserved. Then I found Booktok, and their yummy masked men and bike boys. All I'd needed to do was purchase a few bookshelves and perhaps a thousand dollars' worth of books, funded of course by my OnlyFans page.

I'd attempted to read a couple of the books I'd purchased but it seriously wasn't my thing. It was so much easier to just Google the reviews, watch other girls' TikTok videos, and then fake it. I kept all of my TikTok videos vague in detail and high in cleavage. As a result, I acquired an impressive mix of followers with a high population of fit masked men as well as biketokers.

In saying all this, though, MaskedSurfer was definitely someone I wanted to fuck around with. Smiling to myself, I unlocked my phone.

MASKEDSURFER

Hey beautiful. Ditch the party. Let's smoke. I got the best herb.

VALLEYSMUTTQUEEN

Don't want to share with the others?
That's so rude. Where are you?

MASKEDSURFER

Follow the large stream east a little, till
you get to the end, and there will be a
beautiful lake with a pier. Meet me there,
babe.

VALLEYSMUTTQUEEN

Gross! Don't call me babe. I'll be right
there. Getting high sounds so much
better than Brian trying and failing to get
Lola to like him. Witch probably hexed
the poor guy with some voodoo shit.

I stood, shoving my phone into the front pocket of my Calvin Klein jean overalls, which matched the super cute grey-and-white sports bra and panties I was wearing underneath.

If Brian had any real taste, he'd be paying attention to me, not goth girl. Nothing against Lola. I loved her but, really, what boy in his right mind would choose the strange goth chick with her tarot cards, scary tattoos, and monster dildos over me? I was truly thirty-six but with all the dieting, yoga, and CrossFit, I easily passed for twenty-eight. The cosmetic surgery helped too, of course. Men cared way less about the odd grey hair or age line when you had a large pair of perfect tits to shake in their face.

Walking off in the direction I was told, I pulled out my iPhone and used its flashlight to guide me. I cursed under my breath at each mysterious sound coming from the woods. I was definitely not an *outdoors* kinda girl. Vegas would have been such a better venue. I let out a shudder, my breath creating a cloud in front of me.

Fuck, why didn't I bring a hoodie? I would just have to steal Robert's.

After nearly ten minutes of walking, I finally reached the lake before spotting the small boathouse and pier. I stepped out of the tree line, the moonlit-sky illuminating the clearing perfectly. I cut off the flashlight and slipped my phone back into the pocket of my overalls. With my arms hugging my chest and my hands rubbing at the skin there, attempting to warm myself, I stepped onto the pier.

"Robert?" I called out when I didn't spot him. I did smell weed, though. Bastard better not have started without me. I did not walk through the disgusting woods in the cold for nothing. "Robert, where the fuck are you?" I called out once more as I approached the door to the boathouse, opened it, and stepped inside.

The door creaked loudly on its hinges as it swung open. The room was dark and smelled of lake water, mold, and dust.

"Robert?" I called out while pressing the door closed. An eerie creaking sound rose from behind me, urging me to turn back around. "Fuck!" I cursed when an imposing masked figure appeared in front of me.

"Hello, Barbie," was the last thing I heard before I saw the backside of a large splitting-axe swinging towards me.

12

LYNDSEY

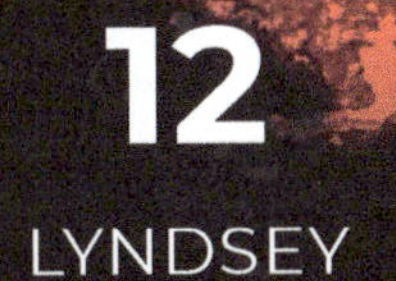

The world around me seemed to move in jerking motions, but my sense of vision and speech were not responding. Everything felt so heavy—throbbing and numb at the same time. Like waking up from the strongest anesthesia after I'd gotten my tits done for the first time.

I attempted to move my body but I couldn't, my biceps and thighs bound to something hard beneath me. However, I wasn't totally supported. The center of my back felt as if it were suspended midair, my spine arching as much as my restraints would allow.

"What a filthy slut you are, my dear." I heard someone speaking in a funny accent. Or was that just an illusion caused by the headache?

"Hey, boys, want me to rate your thick cock? Subscribe to my OnlyFans to get a rating, then stick around to see where I'd like you to stick me, Daddy—*you've got to be fucking kidding me.*"

Something hard hit the ground. I looked up and then back down to see the blurry image of a figure between my legs.

I was naked!

My eyes flicked over my surroundings. I was attached to the boat lift. Thick white zip ties binding my body in a partially-suspended state over the filthy-smelling lake water while some strange masked man with a cheap James Bond accent was stroking himself in front of me.

"What the actual fuck, Robert! This isn't funny! Let me the fuck go, you little-dicked bitch!" I screamed out, struggling against my restraints but it was no use. I wasn't going anywhere.

My eyes locked on to him, my chest heaving with panicked breaths. I watched in horror as he stepped closer to me and felt his fingertips brush up and down my bare pussy, which was dryer than the Sahara.

"What the fuck! Aren't you whores supposed to love this shit? You should be dripping for me right now," he said with an unmistakable hint of frustration. By the looks of it, my lack of arousal was causing him a lot of erectile issues.

"Sorry, buddy, but tiny, flaccid dicks don't really do it for me. You should see the monsters I've fucked in LA. Seriously, Robert, let me fucking down. Was this your attempt at a dark romance reenactment? You can't even get it up. Let me go!" All the noise was just making my head throb even more.

"My dick isn't tiny!" I heard him scream as he slammed his fist down on something mounted to the pillar beside him.

What the fuck did he just hit?

Before I knew it, I was being lowered towards the water. Fear overtook me. This wasn't a game any longer. Robert was seriously on some fucked-up drugs or something. I kicked and screamed as loud as I could. The bottoms of my feet caught the wooden deck floor, the mechanisms faltering as my muscles tensed, resisting the machine's goal to drop me into the lake.

"Robert, let me go! Please, this isn't fucking funny!" I yelled at the figure as he stepped away. He turned back around, dragging something metal behind him. I could hear it scraping across the flooring.

"Shut up and hold still," he said, lifting my phone to my face to unlock it—*it wasn't like I could formulate words anyway.*

My eyes darted from my trembling legs to him as he continued to aim the phone at my face with the flash on.

The fuck-stick was recording me.

"Is this some weird horror fetish from one of your stupid porno books? You guys are all so fucked up." I cursed at him, finally able to scream out a few words as the strain in my legs grew unbearable.

"Bloody hell," he said, letting out a sigh and raising what must have been dragging along the floor.

My eyes locked on to the axe, now poised in the air over the masked man's head. Before I had the opportunity to blink or scream or pray, the blade came down. At first, the pain was instant, like the flip of a switch. What followed seemed to slow down as I heard, felt, and smelled every sensation one at a time. The distinct sound of bones and tendons snapping and popping as my right leg came apart beneath the sharpened edge. I looked down just in time to see my left leg falter and fold upward like a closing book, the back of my knee breaking open as the boat lift resumed my descent.

Warm liquid ran down what remained of my legs, from the breaks at my knees and between my thighs. I didn't even realize I'd been screaming until I tasted the murky lake water and began choking as my body slowly went under.

Looking up at the shadowy figure through the dark haze, I watched as he removed his mask and dipped the head of the axe into the water. He hooked the side of one of my breasts with the bite of the blade and yanked it upward, slicing me open, but I couldn't scream anymore.

The last thing I heard *not Robert* say was, "You know, this entire time, I'd wondered if you'd actually go under with so much Botox and silicone. Science."

Then he was gone, and so was I.

13

SERA

Monday's plan of spending the day making content and going live as a group had practically gone all to pot. Apparently, Robert had had a family emergency that required him to leave suddenly without so much as even saying goodbye. The really odd thing was we'd all woken up to a message from Lyndsey in the Discord saying she'd decided to go with him for emotional support.

James didn't seem to care much about Robert's absence, but I could tell something about Lyndsey's departure was bothering him. She clearly intended on coming back, though, because she'd left her luggage. We'd each tried calling them in Discord without any response. I couldn't say I was particularly fond of Robert, but I had nothing against him at the same time. It did, however, increase Brian's chances with Lola or any of the other ladies—so there was that.

By the time everyone had woken up, it was around noon and half the day was lost. James and I had been up since eight. He'd woken me up with his face between my thighs, licking my pussy as if it were his only purpose in life. Needless to say, I'd orgasmed and then returned the favor as best I could.

It was true what they said, you know. *Everything was bigger in Texas.*

After our morning activities, James and I ate breakfast, then went for a walk along the stream that ran behind the cabin. He was dressed in jeans and a black-and-red flannel, topped off with a straw cowboy hat.

I was starting to want one too.

It was a peaceful walk. We'd both left our phones behind. In part because we didn't want to be disturbed but also due to the fact that without the Wi-Fi at the cabin, there was practically no cell signal. The only solid way of communicating with the outside world, apart from the internet, was the landline phone in the kitchen.

The fresh mountain air was a stark contrast to the muggy city air of Leeds I'd been used to my entire life. Here it was crisp, chilled and invigorating, with a special purity to it.

Breathing in through my nose, I couldn't help but notice how the scent wasn't all too different from James. Strong traces of pine, moss, and damp soil accompanied by the various wild flowers along the stream's edge that hadn't yet wilted or died off with the approaching winter. This was exactly what I'd needed. I was starting to feel rejuvenated, and when I glanced down to where James' large calloused hand was laced with mine, my heart swelled with joy and the hope of a brighter future. Not just for me but perhaps for Alexander as well.

"Is it like this where you live?" I asked, looking away from the towering trees around us and back to James's strong features, noticing the faintest trace of white starting in his beard.

"Not too far off. A lot flatter, though, and more green. Most of the land's cleared off too, of course, but there're plenty of woods surrounding the ranch. You'd like it—I think. Real peaceful. My grandad and Pa built a man-made pond." James paused at the sound of a twig snapping somewhere in the distance. A moment later, he shook his head and continued on. "Pa and I would fish it now and then. We keep it stocked with catfish. Some of them have gotten bigger than my arm, regular sea monsters."

The smile that took over his face as James spoke about fishing with his father betrayed his tough-guy demeanor, revealing the little boy within. Part of me felt a pang of guilt at his mention of his late father. From what James had told me, both his parents had passed away in a fire only a month before this trip. I was honestly surprised when he said he was still attending.

But right now, his face carried no pain. In fact, he was smiling and it made me smile in return.

"That sounds nice. I've never been fishing before. I can't imagine touching a fish like that but I'd love to go along with you."

"They don't fish 'cross the pond?" He looked down at me, adding a teasing tone to his words.

"City girl, remember? And yes, of course, we do. I just don't. My mother and father are very much the prim and proper sort." I could not help but giggle at the image of my parents standing beside a murky river in their very posh suit and dress, trying to wrestle some large river monster out of the water on a fishing line.

"What's so funny, princess?" James said, clearly aware he'd missed out on some inside joke.

"Oh, just imagining my parents doing something as simple as fishing. They can't stand the littlest bit of dirt in the house. I imagine even seeing a fish come out of the water would send them both into a panic—a tragedy." My giggle turned into a full-on laugh and was soon accompanied by a baritone chuckle. The first time I'd genuinely heard this man laugh in person.

"Oh boy, don't reckon they'd take a liking to me then. 'Least not off the cuff," he said. His eyes looking from me back to the path in front of us.

At the sight of his smile, my arms tightened around his without thought. "I *reckon* they would come to see you as a proper gentleman and love you just the same, no matter how rugged you are," I said, trying to imitate his cowboy drawl and failing miserably, which had him laughing again.

Before I knew it, we were stepping out of the forest to a lovely-looking boathouse and pier.

"Oh, this is beautiful and look across the lake! There must be a few more cabins out here too. I bet this is all so stunning in the winter when it snows. I wonder if the lake freezes enough to skate on."

"Likely does. At this elevation, I imagine it gets pretty cold up here," James said as he paused at the door to the boathouse, opening it and peeking inside. "Shame, no boat in the lift. Would have been nice to go out on the water." Shutting the door, he smiled at me.

We walked all the way to the end of the pier and took a seat on the small wooden bench that looked over the lake. His strong arm wrapped around me, and my body melted into his.

"So, this is what peace and happiness feel like," I whispered, peering up and kissing the side of his neck just beneath his beard.

His body tensed. "Careful, Harps. You'll start a stampede, kissing me like that." His voice came out low and gravelly yet dripping with honey, and I wanted every drop.

"Then saddle up, cowboy." I breathed against his neck, placing another kiss on his skin, the sandalwood scent of his beard oil the most intoxicating fragrance I'd ever smelled.

That was all it took. I could feel the heat building between the apex of my thighs. I didn't have the chance to pull back before a strong hand gripped my side and his arm tightened around my shoulders, tugging me closer. I let out a yip as I was then yanked on top of him in a straddling position, his right hand reaching up and closing around my throat and his full lips crashing against mine when he drew me forward. His other hand slipped under my hoodie and shirt, gripping on to my side, covering it from stomach to back.

"Fuck, baby girl, I need you more than the air in my lungs. Right now," he growled as he tugged on my lower lip with his teeth.

My hands moved from his shoulders to the base of my top, and I pulled the hoodie and his T-shirt off in one motion, exposing my chest to him. An offering I knew he wouldn't refuse.

"Fucking take me, Mustang, right here. Please fuck me!" Instinctively, I began grinding on his lap, becoming aware of the fact I was soaking through my trousers.

The morning air was chilly against my bare chest, making the sensation of his mouth sucking one of my nipples even more exhilarating. A moan escaped my lips and I swiped off his cowboy hat, placing it on my own head so I could grip the back of his, lacing my fingers together over his hair. He bit my nipple, rotating it between his teeth before moving to the other breast while cupping the first one and kneading it firmly.

"Fuck, James, *Sir*, please bite it harder."

He answered my prayer as I continued to grind on him. Fully aware of how hard his cock was beneath me. James began a pattern of kissing over my breasts, moving from one to the other. Caressing, biting, and licking my nipples. Ensuring to give the other one the proper attention with his fingers till his mouth returned to it.

It might have been fifteen degrees Celsius, but it might as well have been the dead of summer. I was sweating and my breathing was getting harder as the inferno that was my arousal threatened to erupt in a pleasantly-violent climax—an occurrence that had happened only once before.

For a split second, I considered stopping, fearing how James would react. But fuck, it felt too good.

Removing one hand from the back of his head, I gripped the arm of the bench, using it as support as I leaned back so I could grind against his hard cock at a better angle. His body tensed reflexively beneath me. He was fighting the urge to thrust.

Fucking hell, this man knew what he was doing. If he were to begin thrusting up into me, he could very well throw off the rhythm I was building.

"Fuck, Jame—" was all I got out as my body locked up, before shaking violently as my arousal erupted in a warm, wet, pleasurable release.

I almost let go of the bench, but his hand moved to my upper back to support me, preventing me from falling. Both of our trousers were certainly soaked now. As that realization hit me, I felt my cheeks redden with concern and slight embarrassment, instead of pleasure.

Would he be disgusted?

I'd done research after the first time I'd accidentally discovered I could "squirt." And that research had told me many things, including the fact that some lovers thought it was gross.

Leaning forward again, I lowered my eyes to James's face and what I saw stoked the heat between my thighs all over again. Pure lust was staring back at me. His eyes had gone dark. Unhinged. As if something feral had been uncaged.

I opened my mouth to apologize, but the guttural growl that rose from his throat disconnected my brain.

14

JAMES

I'd felt her heat building up steadily since I pulled her onto me, but the warm torrential downpour that had erupted from her body had baptized me in her passion, washing away all my restraint. I gripped Sera beneath her ass and stood, lifting her body with me.

My eyes locked on to her as I turned and set her down on the bench, then positioned myself in front of her. My jeans were soaked with her release, my cock pressing painfully against the restricting denim. Slowly, I reached down and undid my large western buckle, and with a whip of my fist, ripped my belt from the loops of my jeans, the leather snapping as it came free.

"Such a dirty girl, so hot for my cock. Undo my fly and show me how badly you crave it." I began folding the belt in my hands without ever taking my eyes off her.

She hesitated for the briefest of moments before beginning to work my jeans with her delicate fingers. Fumbling at first, she struggled with the button but her mouth opened eagerly as she got the zipper down and pulled the fabric, along with my briefs, down to my knees. My cock springing into action once freed.

"Like what you see? Go ahead… worship my cock with your mouth. Make me proud," I said as I flexed my cock, making it bounce and smack against her lips as soon as she moved closer.

Her delicate hands closed around my shaft, one palm on top of the other, leaving the head exposed. I looked down, watching as Sera brushed her mouth over my cock, kissing it softly before closing her lips around the tip. Giving it warm, wet kisses before taking the entire head in her pretty mouth. Her tongue darted out, making slow circles as her hands stroked me.

Seeing a strand of her hair fall down onto her cheek, I collected her hair into a ponytail, gripping it tightly. Then, with my free hand, I pulled the adjustable bracelet she'd gifted me for my birthday over my fist and placed it around her hair. Cinching it closed. It was the first time I'd taken it off.

Sera shifted her top hand, allowing herself to take me deeper into her mouth while grabbing onto my ass instead.

"Fuck, that's it, baby girl. Open your eyes. Keep them locked on me as you worship my cock."

She did as she was told, those breathtaking obsidian pools sending surges of lightning through my entire body. My muscles seeming to flex then relax and my skin burning like I'd taken too much pre-workout. This woman unlocked levels of desire in me that I didn't think were possible. She was all-consuming. I would wage war, move mountains, burn cities to the ground if that was what it took to ensure I got to look into these eyes every day for the rest of my mortal existence. Death would have to take us both at once if he wanted her. On the other hand, if I were to die before she did, I would kill the devil himself to come back just to be with her again.

Sera's lips parted, her hand sliding over my shaft to collect her saliva and work it around my cock, enabling her palm to glide up and down after she resealed her mouth over the top.

"You work my cock so nicely, baby girl," I groaned out, instinct driving me to tilt my head back and moan in pleasure.

But I refused to take my eyes off hers. "I want to see how much of me you can really take, baby girl. Nice and slow, all the way down."

Her hand shifted from the hilt of my shaft to cup my balls, as she took my cock deeper into her throat. She almost got all of it inside, but began to struggle with the last half inch.

She tried to pull her head back, but I held her in place. "No, no, stay right there. Breathe through your nose and relax. That's my good girl…"

She'd really done such a good job, but I couldn't hold back anymore. I pulled my hips away, then thrust forward into her throat. By the time she started to gag and sputter on my cock, I'd already pulled away again and was thrusting forward for a second time. Her hands flailed till they found purchase on my ass, her nails digging into me. Making me drive forward harder. She tried to maintain eye contact, even as tears began to form and glisten on her cheeks.

"You look so beautiful with my cock in your mouth, baby girl," I said in a praising tone that betrayed the brutality of my actions. My eyes honed in on one tear running down her cheek, my hips thrusting faster and harder. Only stopping when I saw it meet her lips. The next time I drew back, I pulled all the way out, my cock dripping with her saliva.

Sera gasped. "Fuck!"

"I told you to breathe through your nose." I shook my head as I stepped back, slowly stroking myself while kicking off my boots and moving out of my jeans. "Strip," I commanded.

Sera paused, as if just now remembering that we were standing at the end of a pier in broad daylight.

"Eyes on me. Don't worry if anyone sees us. I'll let them watch me make you come on my cock. Then I'll kill them."

Her eyes went wide but not with fear, more like lust. My little harpy liked the idea of being watched. Of me killing for her.

She stepped out of her shoes, then removed her jeans and panties.

"Good. Now kneel on the bench. Hold on tight to the back."

She did as I commanded. And fuck, the view in front of me was the only thing that might have gotten me to believe in some greater being. Her pussy was perfect and quite literally dripping wet. I opened my hand enough to let the belt drop so that it was folded in half, my palm tightly gripping the buckle and the end.

"You blinked four times, and you forgot to breathe properly." I smiled behind her. Knowing that deep down, she was fucking loving this. I let the leather brush over her ass. "That's five whippings."

"Fuck, James…" she said, through heavy pants, her voice sweet and trembling with desire.

"Hush. Do you remember your safe word?" I asked.

"Red," she replied.

"Red, *what*?"

"Red, Sir."

"Good girl. Now count them out."

Before she had the chance to say anything else, I cocked the belt back and let loose, whipping it across the beautiful fullness of her milky-white ass. The leather cracked against her skin, and she gasped.

"Count, Sera!" I demanded.

"One," she whimpered.

I continued the process, being sure to get both cheeks equally, not wishing to cause an uneven amount of damage.

"Two… three… four…"

Her thighs were trembling, and I caught a glimpse of tears falling from her face. I paused, waiting to see if she would use her safe word and put an end to this. But it never came.

She kneeled on the bench, her body shaking and her eyes dripping with tears as her pussy *dripped* with her arousal. My girl was fucking feral for it, and I was so proud of her.

"Five! Thank you, Sir.." She was slumping slightly, but she never let go of the bench, just like I'd instructed her.

I tossed my belt on top of my jeans and dropped to my knees behind her. Her full ass now decorated with red welts and a few small breaks in the skin from two stronger strikes. Gently, I placed my hands on the sides of her thighs and began to kiss every inch of her raised flesh. She winced a time or two, but the next few moments passed in mostly silence. Nothing but the sounds of our breathing and the water below the pier.

Once I'd kissed every mark I'd given her, I kissed her dripping pussy, then ran my tongue up her core, collecting all her delicious arousal on my tongue as I stood. Gliding my hands to her hips, I aligned my cock with her pussy, moving forward as the tip slipped into her with ease, despite how tightly she hugged me.

"Don't let go," was the only warning I gave her before relentlessly thrusting into her, to the point the wooden bench creaked and threatened to splinter.

Sera took me so well. She was fucking made for me. The perfect blend of elegance and ferocity. *My harpy.*

With each drive of my hips, she slowly lowered her chest till it was pressed against the back of the bench, giving her ass to me so nicely. I wasn't going to last very long after all the foreplay. *That*, mixed with the fact anyone could be watching me fuck my harpy right now, had me especially hard. I refused to come before she did, though. My girl needed to know that I—and only I—could or would ever give her such pleasure.

"I want you to come on my cock for me like the good fucking girl you are, Sera. You're going to have to get used to this, because this is what every single day of the rest of your life is going to be like. Me fucking your tight hole like you're my personal fuck toy." I gritted my teeth, growling out the words as I thrusted harder and harder, ensuring I maintained a set rhythm.

"James, yes, please. I'm yours, fucking yours!" she moaned out. "Oh god."

"No! You pray to me. My name is the only one you are allowed to cry out!" I cocked my hand back and slapped it hard across her ass, that same hand then reaching around to squeeze her throat.

"Yes… Sir…" she huffed, her body beginning to quiver again.

I felt an overwhelming surge of heat on my cock as she came for me. The intensity of the moment triggered my own orgasm, my cock erupting deep inside her. Our bodies seemed to shake in harmony, our nervous systems totally rocked by our orgasms.

Hardly able to keep my legs under me, I had to reach out with my free hand and grab Sera's waist before she collapsed over the bench. Following her momentum and in my own body's apparent failure, I pulled her back to my chest and spun us. My side hit the bench, the edges of the wood biting between my ribs and into my hip. With Sera wrapped in my arms, I turned till she was on my lap, both of us sitting in silence while soaking in the sunlight.

After a few moments, Sera moved to straddle me, our bodies—covered in hot, sweaty passion—becoming one. She wrapped her arms around my neck as our breaths slowly fell in sync. It was the strangest feeling, having her chest pressed against mine. I could swear our hearts were beating as one.

It was then that I felt my mouth open, heard my own voice, but the words I said in that moment came out naturally. Without hesitation or forethought.

"I love you, Sera."

15

SERA

I'd just regained the ability to breathe. I didn't think my hearing was affected, but clearly it was.

Did James just say what I think he said?

I raised my head, about to ask him to repeat himself until I saw his eyes. He'd said it. It was all over his face. His gaze was soft with subtle hints of fear. Fear of rejection. This fire-and-brimstone warrior... This tattooed, muscular, mountain of a man... This living, breathing example of the shadow daddies in the dark romance books we both enjoyed had just dropped all his defenses with those three words. He looked up at me, and I knew I could destroy him if I wanted to. But I didn't want to. This man had been my bedrock practically since we'd met.

It'd almost been a year since we'd started talking. A year since my online masked man crush followed me back, and I was bold enough to sneak into his DMs—after two glasses of pinot grigio to help steel my nerves. I never actually thought he'd respond, though.

Since then, we'd chatted every day. We'd been each other's therapist, cheerleader, best friend, and lover. He'd randomly send me flowers and coffee when I was having a bad day, but in most instances, it was just because he felt like it. Our friends all suspected there was something growing between us but we never confirmed it. I had enough going on, and we'd agreed to meet in person before taking whatever this was to the next level. It was always clear, though. The strongest feelings were the ones we'd never said. Every *good morning* and every *good night* was accompanied by an unspoken *I love you.*

I wasn't sure how long I'd been staring, lost in his eyes, before I replied with, "I love you too, James," leaned forward and pressed my lips to his.

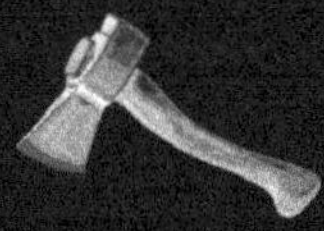

We eventually made our way back to the cabin, a bit earlier than I would have liked, but James had pointed out the fast-moving clouds that were approaching from the north and stated that it was going to rain.

Then we went straight to our room and took a much-needed shower, which resulted in round two when James fucked me up against the tiled wall. When we went downstairs to join the others, we found all four of them in the living room.

Brian was setting up a laptop on the mantle with a ring light camera attached to the top of the screen. The others had moved the couch a little closer and set up some of their own ring lights on the sides to increase the light quality of the room. We'd all brought a few of our favorite books as well as a few we thought we might use for a livestream buddy-read session.

"Well, there you are. Thought perhaps you two had abandoned us too," Brian said, stepping away from the laptop and looking over the rest of the room.

"Don't worry, Brian. I'm sure they've just been off fucking.

Don't pretend we couldn't hear them in the shower." Lola laughed from where she was standing off to the side, a wide selection of liquor bottles lined up on a decorative table beside her. She plucked up the bottle of Fireball and filled six shot glasses before grabbing the silver serving platter beneath them.

"Lola! I said not to comment on that. You're going to make them uncomfortable!" Jade said somewhat louder than her usual speaking voice.

"I doubt they're surprised we heard them, and if I know Mustang, he wanted us to hear them," Danielle replied, letting out a laugh. "Sera and James, you two are perfectly fine. I'm glad you're enjoying yourselves. Next time, invite a girl." She winked at me before adding, "We *have* been waiting on you, though."

"I'm so sorry, everyone. We definitely did not intend for you to hear anything." I could feel the heat rushing to my cheeks and glanced up at James, while the smirk on his face told me he had in fact intended for them to hear us.

He didn't verbalize it. He didn't need to. His body language said it all as his hand reached down to pat me on the ass.

I quickly looked back to the rest of the group, my eyes lingering on Danielle as I pretended I wasn't aroused by his possessiveness. "What are we setting up for?"

Lola stepped forward, presenting us with the tray of shots. "Name the male character. We take turns pulling a piece of paper out of a jar and reading the quote out loud. Everyone then writes their answer on their whiteboard, and when the timer goes off, you flip it over. Get it wrong, you take a shot." She worked her way around the room. "Now, since we can't very well risk doing shots on camera, you'll have to step out of view to take your shot, refill it, and sit back down."

"You sure I can't just take a sip of White Claw?" Jade said, hesitantly taking her shot glass.

"Fuck no," Lola was quick to respond.

"You read more than any of us put together. You have nothing to worry about." Danielle gave Jade a reassuring pat on the back as she took her own glass.

Brian was the last to receive his glass. "Thanks, Lola," he said, grinning from ear-to-ear like a love sick puppy. The poor golden that he was. "Well, how about we all do one to lubricate the gears before we mask up—those of us who need to anyway?" He was clearly trying to sound more macho all while attempting to not look at Lola.

"Now you're talking, golden boy!" Lola said, smacking Brian on the ass and nearly causing him to drop his drink. With that, everyone stood and gathered in front of the fireplace.

"Oh, wait! Let's get this on video. We've barely taken any photos yet!" Danielle called out as she scrambled over to the mantle, propping her phone up on Brian's laptop and hitting the record button.

James's hand gripped my waist tighter. "Good idea. I want to capture as many memories as possible."

Once we were all assembled so that the phone's camera had us all in sight, Lola took it upon herself to utter a toast. "Here's to courage. Here's to honor. If you can't come in her, come on her!"

With that, everyone kicked back their shots, Brian and Jade both coughing as the whiskey made its way down their throats.

On the other hand, the only noise that escaped James was a rumbling laughter. "I haven't heard that one in a while. Good job, Lola."

She winked before she went to fetch the bottle for refills. A twinge of anger flashed through me, but I felt James's hand tighten on my side as if holding me back.

"Come on, Harps. Let's mask up. To the Batcave, Batgirl," he said in a low whisper, turning me towards the stairs.

"Keep it in your pants for at least a few hours, you two!" Lola called after us.

I looked back over a shoulder to see her sculling another shot before Brian's figure blocked her from view as he made his way to his room to get ready for the live.

James and I took our positions in front of the double sinks, each pulling out our own makeup bag. I laughed at the sight of us applying our signature looks in the mirror. James with his easy block of black grease paint from the nose up, versus my elegant eye shadow and cat eye.

"What?" he asked, appearing puzzled by my sudden outburst.

"Oh, just imagining us living together and having to have our own makeup stations."

"Oh yeah, my Mehron and your Kat Von Dee or whatever." He chuckled as he grabbed a liner and cleaned up the area around his eyes, breaking off the tip as he did so.

"Sir, if I ever catch you using my makeup like that, I'll beat you with the dull end of your own axe," I replied as he began packing up his supplies and washing the black from his palms.

"Hah, don't worry, sweetheart. I know better than to mess with any of your cursed war paint." He dried off his hands on a towel and kissed the side of my head before stepping back into the bedroom. "Harps, have you seen my helmet anywhere? I thought I left it on the top shelf of the closet but it's not there?"

"No, I haven't. But shouldn't you stick with the cloth skull face one? It'll make taking shots easier. We both know you're going to be taking a lot of them," I teased, leaning back to glance out the bathroom door. "I'm sure it's somewhere around here. We'll find it after the live. Perhaps it fell and rolled under the bed or something." I stepped out of the bathroom with my mask on and my hair curled into nice, thick, dark waves.

"Yeah right, you wish. Reckon I won't be taking a single one. Really, though, I don't see it anywhere," he called back as I watched him pull his fabric mask down over his face, adjusting it to sit properly before he returned his cowboy hat to the top of his head. "How do I look?" James held out his arms, presenting himself for inspection.

"Hmm, how does that one song go? Save a horse, ride a cowboy?" I walked over, raised myself up on my tiptoes, and kissed him through the fabric of our masks as I reached around to give his ass a squeeze.

Damn, he had a nice one. I wasn't really sure if guys knew this, but there was just something about a man with a nice ass that was damn sexy.

His body tensed and his arms moved in to grab me. The look in his eyes telling me if I let him, he was going to throw me down on the bed and fuck me all over again.

Having been ready for it, though, I put my hand on his chest and took a step back. "The live first, Mr. Mustang. Then I'll find out if I make much of a bronco rider." I winked and lightly grabbed the already apparent bulge in his jeans before turning on my heels. "Put your gun away, cowboy."

Then I darted out the door with the sound of his boots and spurs close behind me, knowing I was playing with fire.

About forty-five minutes later, we were going live. Brian the "MaskedGentleman" had managed to secure a spot at the end of the couch next to Lola, Danielle on her other side, followed by Jade on the loveseat and then *Mustang* with me sitting on his lap. I'd actually attempted to squeeze between them, but James didn't really give me an option. The moment I went to drop down, he grabbed my hips and redirected me onto his lap. Clearly his way of telling all my followers that I was his.

I'd be lying if I said it didn't turn me on.

"All right, Danielle, your go!" Lola stated while passing over the jar of quotes.

So far, we'd done two rounds and the only ones to take a shot were Brian and Danielle. Though Lola was already ahead of the rest of the group having poured a White Claw into her coffee mug to drink on camera. We had our phones set up in front of us, guesting in our own box while Brian hosted on his laptop, announcing that we had fifty viewers observing the chaos.

The comments in the chat were moving so fast it was nearly impossible to keep up, but two names entering at the same time caught my eye. "Oh, Lyndsey and MaskedSurfer just joined us! You two jerks! We've been trying to reach you! Get back here soon before you miss the entire trip!" I said to them, leaning towards my phone as the rest of the group chimed in around me.

Their responses popped up, and Brian read them out loud:

MASKEDSURFER

> Just reconnecting with nature together.
> Out hiking.

VALLEYSMUTTQUEEN

> Not to mention, swimming. You guys will
> have to join us soon.

MASKEDSURFER

> Very soon. Though you all do look so
> cozy.

"What the fuck? Where are you assholes? You're back? Well, get in here and play with us. Stop fucking around." Lola laughed and got up to go take what was likely her fifth shot of the evening.

"They can see us on their screens, girl. They aren't here," Danielle reminded her with a laugh.

Lots of good bottle options you have there. Wish I could join you.

"How's he know that? The alcohol is off camera?" I whispered to James.

My question goes unheard to everyone else. Mostly thanks to Lola crying out, "Fuck yes, we do!"

James shifted me off his lap and into his spot on the sofa. "Wait here," he said, his tone making it clear that it was not up for discussion.

"Yes, Sir," I said on impulse, which caused Jade to turn in my direction with a wide-eyed grin on her face.

A moment later, James returned. He shook his head. "Surfer's car isn't out front, just my truck. He must be fucking around. Let's play."

Then he lifted me up and sat me back down on his lap, and we resumed our game. Though it was obvious we were all keeping an eye on our screens, watching for more comments from Robert or Lyndsey.

None came.

Danielle adjusted herself in her seat, setting her board on the ground by her feet before taking the jar. "All right then, let's get a good one," she said as she reached her hand inside, shuffling around a bit before pulling out a piece of paper. She unfolded it and a wicked smirk appeared on her face. "This is a damn good one. *Only now she's—*"

A loud boom of thunder shook the entire cabin to the point the water in my glass on the coffee table reminded me of the first *Jurassic Park* film.

The roar made me jump, and I could have very easily fallen off James's lap but he'd gripped me tighter, pinning me down on him.

"Fuck!" Jade cried out beside us.

I glanced out the window, and it was as if that thunder clap had torn open the sky. Just as James had predicted, it was down-pouring. I was too distracted by everything going on inside to notice when it started. But now there was no missing it. You could hear the intensity of the rain assaulting the cabin. A flash of lightning illuminated the windows, eliciting yet another scream from Jade and this time Brian as well.

I felt the quick rise and fall of James's chest as he attempted to suppress himself. But at a second boom of thunder, he couldn't hold back any longer and his laughter filled the room. Lola joined in and soon everyone was cackling. Including our viewers.

LOL!

Ha-ha-ha!

OMG, was that MaskedGentleman squealing!?

"I think that's a sign for us all to take another shot!" Brian declared, standing and holding a hand up to the laptop screen. "One moment, everyone." He then made his way over to the liquor table. Without question, the rest of us followed his lead.

"That was fucking wild timing. Brian, I want something better than the Fireball, though. Pour me a Jameson," Danielle said, closing in on the table.

Another brilliant flash of lightning filled the windows, trailed by multiple booms. But none of the thunderclaps were nearly as loud as the scream that erupted from Jade's throat. She stumbled backwards, tripping over her own feet, and would have likely crashed to the floor had James not been quick to move behind her.

"Whoa, easy there, darlin'. It's only thunder," he said in that soothing voice of his.

"Fuck no! A face! There was a fucking guy or monster outside the window!" she shrieked, pointing towards the sliding glass doors. The same ones James had appeared in front of on our first night here.

16

JAMES

I hadn't seen anything myself, but Jade didn't seem the type to hallucinate and she wasn't drunk yet either.

"Stay here. I'll check it out. I'm sure it was nothing. Just the weather playing tricks on your mind," I said in an attempt to comfort her. I patted her on the shoulder before stepping past the others. Brian motioned towards the door as if he intended to join me, but I held up a hand before he had the chance. "Stay here with the girls. Do your shot and get back to the live. I'll just take a look around and be right back."

"Be careful, James!" Jade cried out.

I peered over a shoulder to see Sera handing Jade a shot while rubbing at the girl's shoulder. Our eyes locked, and I recognized the concern painted on her face. I gave her a wink and turned away before she could tell me to stay inside.

Sliding open the door, I stepped out into the storm. The rain was practically sideways in the wind, cutting through my hoodie like razor blades. I held up my hand, shielding my eyes as I scanned the area. The growing darkness of the night made it near impossible to see much farther than the perimeter of the cabin between the frequent flashes of lightning.

Back home, this sort of storm would immediately raise concerns about tornados as we sat around the ranch, waiting for the sirens to start wailing. But this wasn't a tornado zone.

I slowly crossed the deck to peer over the railing, but all I saw was the outer grounds of the cabin now being assaulted by the rain. When I reached the top of the stairs, something finally caught my eye. A set of muddy footprints trailing up and down the wooden steps. Apart from a few thicker clods of dirt, the prints quickly vanished as they washed away in the rain.

Fuck, someone was out there.

"Robert, you fuck…" It had to be him or some lost hunter, or maybe the owner was a creep and wanted to see what his guests were doing. Anything was possible but my mind kept pulling back to the idea of a pissed-off Robert camping out somewhere in the woods, perhaps joined now by Lyndsey, trying to play tricks on us.

I started carefully down the stairs, my eyes darting along every surface as soon as my feet hit the landing. Including the area beneath the deck against the house, out into the tree line, and then over to the water's edge. There was no one in sight but what I did find were more sunken pits filling with rain in the shape of footprints, leading away from the stairs towards the stream.

"Well, fuck…"

Whoever this was had the common sense enough to cover their tracks. They knew how to avoid being followed. This made me doubt it could be Robert, as he didn't seem too high on the common-sense scale. However, I knew better than to underestimate anyone. There was one other possibility that had crossed my mind. A possibility that would escalate the situation far worse than any stupid prank.

Point was, they were gone now and any attempt to try to

pick up the tracks on the other side of the stream was useless in this weather.

A muffled chorus of screams came from behind me. I glanced back and noticed that the interior of the cabin had gone dark. I spun around and realized that every light both inside and outside had gone off. Not surprising given the storm, but pair it up with our mystery guest and I wasn't taking any chances.

I did my due diligence, though, and made a 360-security check around the perimeter. Hopefully, the storm would pass and the power would be restored or perhaps the owner had a backup generator somewhere on the property. Surely the boathouse. As I approached the sliding glass door, it slid open, revealing Sera, who was holding her phone's flashlight in my direction.

"Thank God! I was getting worried. Come inside!" she called out, raising her voice to combat another clap of thunder.

I stepped past her and she slammed the door shut before throwing a towel around me. She instantly began trying to dry me off. "I'm fine and way too wet for just the towel, but thank you, baby girl," I told her.

She smiled and raised up on her toes to plant a kiss against my wet lips. I peered over the top of her head and saw multiple flashes of light dance across the walls, accompanied by the sounds of cupboards opening and shutting as the rest of the group tried to navigate the cabin with the help of their cellphones.

"Found some!" Jade called out from the kitchen, and a moment later, she emerged with a handful of candles pinned to her chest. "James! Thank God you're back inside. Was anyone out there?" She placed a few candles around us. Then Danielle appeared behind her, a lighter in hand, and with their combined efforts, the room was well enough illuminated.

"Nothing but the storm. Though I'm afraid it may be some time before the power returns. Up in the mountains like this, the power lines are typically above ground, meaning someone will have to locate and fix them," I answered, stepping over and taking a candle from her arms. "Thanks for finding these. I suggest everyone bed down for the night. And be sure to put your phone's battery saver on."

"Danielle and I were thinking maybe we should all just camp out here in the living room. Could be a lot safer..." Jade's expression was pleading, her voice laced with fear.

Before Sera or I had a chance to respond, Lola and Brian returned with another handful of unlit candles from downstairs. "Found some more. I think the idea of us all camping out here sounds fun. There's plenty of space. James and I can bring up a couple of the mattresses, and between those and the couches, we'll be set," he said.

Lola quickly parted from Brian and plopped onto the couch. "Right, well, dibs on this one." She smiled brightly, a hard contrast to Brian's frown.

I shook my head and chuckled. Keeping my thoughts to myself, which were along the lines of how he looked like a wounded puppy. That boy was head over heels for our resident goth girl, and it was getting sadder and sadder as time went on.

"Oh, that does sound fun!" Sera said, to my dismay. I didn't want to share her presence with the others for the remainder of the night. I had every intention of fucking her as much as possible before this trip was over. "Doesn't it?" She beamed up at me, those big doe eyes breaking down my hard outer shell.

"Loads," I replied.

"Well, first thing's first. I need to get out of these cold, wet clothes before I catch my death. And have a hot shower." I look to Brian, locking eyes with the man. "How about we grab one of those mattresses from downstairs first? We can take Robert's."

"Yeah, mate. You don't want to shower and change first?" he asked.

"No, let's get the girls situated as quickly as possible," I said, before turning to Sera. I kissed her on the forehead. "Harps, I saw some extra blankets and pillows in the closet near the front door."

"Of course," she responded like the good girl she was and, taking Jade with her, headed in that direction.

Not long after, Brian and I were downstairs, folding up Robert's bedding. I pinned him with a glare. "I need to tell you something but you need to keep a cool head. Do you understand?"

"Yeah, mate, what is it?"

"Someone's out there. I believe Jade was right when she said she saw a face. When I went outside, I spotted what I'm pretty sure were muddy footprints coming up the stairs and then back down, leading to the creek. Not sure what else it could have been." I paused, watching Brian's face, curious as to how he'd react. The guy wasn't exactly alpha male material. He sold insurance for a living, and I was fairly confident he'd never been in a true high-stress situation before.

To his credit, the only sign of nerves I could detect was a slight twitch of his jaw. "Robert, you suppose? His message about the liquor in the TikTok live would make sense then. Think he's out there trying to spook us? Perhaps holding a grudge for you kicking his teeth in?"

"It's one possibility. Either way, just keep your wits about you. I'd ease up on the drinking tonight. Try to keep the girls where you can see them, and for fuck's sake, don't let Lola take any more shots. Best they all bed down. You and I will go around the cabin, ensure everything is locked, and pull all the blinds and curtains closed."

"Better safe than sorry, right?" Brian said. "In that case, let's get everything sorted quickly."

With a nod, I picked up the mattress on my own and directed Brian to grab the bedding. I didn't need help with a full-size. I just needed a passable excuse to get him alone for a few minutes.

Rejoining the women on the main floor, we moved the coffee table out farther and set the mattress down in the center. Between the two couches, the loveseat, the lounger, and the mattress, there would be enough room for the four of them to sleep comfortably. I had no intention of staying here with Sera. Brian would be able to keep an eye on the girls on his own just fine. And the sounds in this cabin carried well enough away that if there were any disturbances, we'd likely hear it upstairs, despite the storm.

"I'll grab a few more pillows and be back," Brian said before heading downstairs as cover for what he was really doing, which was ensuring the doors and windows were secured. He returned a few minutes later, offering a subtle nod of his head.

The girls continued their conversation around the liquor table, not paying either of us guys any mind. Besides Lola, who was sitting on the couch she'd claimed earlier. A White Claw in one hand, the other beneath the blanket as she stared at me.

The woman had made multiple attempts to hit on me in the past, going as far as sending unsolicited videos on Snapchat. I'd eventually had to delete her on the app for her to get the message. But judging by the way she was biting her lip and looking at me right now, my guess was she hadn't given up.

I turned my back and shook my head before I grabbed some kindling and firewood from the rack beside the fireplace. The added warmth would likely help the girls relax as well as provide some illumination till it died out. But by then, I expected all would be asleep.

As I brought the lighter to the kindling, I heard Lola call out from behind me. "Oh, that's a great idea, James. You're going to make it so nice and warm in here." She laughed, slurring her words.

I glanced over a shoulder to see that she'd pulled the blanket higher on her lap. Her legs spread wide beneath the fabric. It was hard to make out what she was doing. At the same time, it was no mystery. She was holding her shorts off to the side, as the fingers of her free hand worked up and down her slit. Her eyes burning into me, drunk as they were.

Any other man would leap at the open invitation to fuck her. Brian would be the first in line. Perhaps he would get lucky tonight after all. Me, on the other hand? All I felt was disgust. Not only because of how pathetic I thought it was, but also because I wanted one woman and one woman only, and she was in the room with us.

I turned back towards the fire and spat into the flames, my repulsion so strong it needed some sort of release. "Right then, I should shower and get out of these clothes," I said, gritting my teeth as I pushed up and made my way over to where Sera stood at the liquor table.

I had half a mind to call Lola out, but she was drunk. I could continue to ignore her advances just fine. It wasn't worth causing dissention within the ranks. She'd sober up, and her hangover would be enough of a punishment tomorrow.

"Right, yes. Let's get you into a nice, hot shower. Girls, we'll be back in a bit!" Sera said, accepting my arm and picking up one of the candles.

I grabbed a candle of my own before looking to Brian. "Don't wait up, and don't let Lola drink anymore," I commanded softly.

"Got it, mate."

17

As soon as we entered the bedroom, James went to the door that opened up to the small private patio overlooking the cabin's front entrance. He leaned his head out, allowing the chilled air and rain to blow inside before quickly shutting the door, ensuring the lock was in place and pulling the blackout curtains closed.

"You seem on edge. What is it?" I dared to ask, with a measure of concern in my voice.

He turned back towards me and my stomach tensed at the expression I saw on his face—or perhaps at the lack of emotion. His features were hard. His brows furrowed and his eyes appearing laser focused yet distant at the same time, as if he wasn't looking at me but through me.

"James?"

With the sound of his name, he seemed to come back from wherever he was just now. "Ah, sorry. Guess I zoned out there for a minute. I'm going to get in the shower," he said, stepping over to me and kissing my forehead, then taking one of the candles with him before disappearing into the bathroom.

A moment later, I heard the sound of the shower turning on. He hadn't invited *or commanded* me to join him. Something was definitely off. This man had done a damn good job of fucking me every chance he got the entire time we'd been here. The fact he wasn't bending me over in the shower right now was concerning. He'd said there wasn't anything outside when he'd checked, but since then, he'd seemed all business. Perhaps he was just tired and cold from being caught in the storm?

I pulled my phone from my pocket and considered sending my parents a text and video for Alexander. Only to unlock my screen and frown, coming to the realization that in addition to having no signal, the Wi-Fi was out.

Of course it was. No power meant no internet.

"First world problems." I sighed and turned on the airplane mode and battery saver to keep the device alive for as long as possible.

Going to my side of the bed, I plugged my phone in so that when the power did hopefully return, it would be ready to charge. I remembered seeing a few tea candles in the nightstand drawer and decided to be spontaneous. I pulled out a handful and placed them around the room, lighting the wick as I went till the space was delicately illuminated.

A deafening boom of thunder caused the glass patio door to rattle as if someone were trying to force it open. And I jumped, a squeal escaping my lips. Shaking my head at myself, I looked to the bathroom door, at a loss for what to do. That was until my eyes drifted over to the bed. More specifically, to one of the restraints currently dangling from the corner of the bedhead. A smile tugged at my mouth as I moved to the dresser and grabbed the outfit I'd bought specifically for this trip.

I stripped down and then proceeded to put on the black lace teddy, the thigh garters, and the crotchless gusset with thin gold chains lacing the front together just below my breasts and deco-rating the shoulder strap. James had no idea I'd bought this for him, and I been wondering if I'd even be able to work up the courage to wear it.

Stepping over to the mirror to see my reflection, I was surprised by the woman looking back at me. Her light skin and many elegant tattoos complemented by the black lace lingerie. She looked sexy and powerful, a woman in charge, yet beautiful and fragile at the same time. The image had the heat growing between my thighs.

Fuck, I was turning myself on.

The shower cut off, and I realized I had one chance to do this right. On first instinct, I lifted my arm. Setting my hand against the door while leaning with my other hand on my hip.

No, fuck! That was the book boyfriend lean. Stupid!

Quickly righting myself, I grabbed one of James's belts hanging on the back of the door, folded it in half, and moved closer to the foot of the bed, where the storage chest was located. Then I braced one foot on top and faced the bathroom, gripping the ends of the belt and resting the length of it on the open palm of my free hand.

The bathroom door opened with all the dramatization of a WWE superstar entrance. Steam rolled out, the candlelight flickering as James exited. His skin glowed warm and orange in the light, a few beads of water glistening on his chest before falling towards the towel wrapped around his waist. It took him a moment to see me as he dried his beard. His glare settling on me in a predatory gaze as soon as he lowered the material from his face. He scanned all the way down to where my core was exposed between my thighs, slowly bringing his hungry eyes back to meet mine.

"Fuck, Harps, you look amazing." He took a long step forward, his hands outstretched. And right before he was able to make contact, I pressed the folded belt against the center of his chest.

"Down boy..." I heard the hesitation in my own voice but it

didn't seem to matter. He listened anyway, his brows rising in surprise. A smile separated his full lips and he chuckled.

"Oh, this is unexpected. Going to show me your claws, little harpy?" His tone was teasing, almost daring. He was challenging me and something about that added fuel to my fire.

I cocked a hand back, the leather of the folded belt cracking against his cheek. His head turned with the blow, and for a brief moment, I froze. I'd never struck a man before, not in any sort of way. And I'd certainly never tried dominating my partner, but I'd read about it. I had watched scenes on Pornhub and gotten off to it. Doing it for real, though? That was next level.

James let out a hiss, and I tensed.

Fuck, did I take it too far?

But when his face turned back, I realized he was smiling. "Harder," was all he said. His eyes dark and piercing. Like a pair of obsidian daggers plunging into me. Into my desire. He was a feral lion and I was his tamer.

"Sit," I commanded, dropping my foot from the chest and pointing downward with the folded belt.

When James didn't immediately respond, I grabbed his shoulders and guided him over till his heels were against the chest. Then I shoved him back. The towel in his hands falling to the floor while the one wrapped around his waist split open between his legs, just barely exposing the dark ink of his inner thigh tattoos.

I stood over him, my glare locking on to the radiant forest-green of his eyes. And the things I found there? The desire, the rage, and something darker—something I couldn't find a name for. They made my core ignite.

Turning away from him, I sauntered across the room, hearing "Goddess" by Written by Wolves playing in my head. My body was perfectly framed in the dresser's mirror, James's reflection showing each time I swayed far enough to one side or the other. His eyes honed in on my ass. I could practically feel them on me.

I moved the belt behind me and unfolded it, pulling it tight against the skin under my ass. Then I bent at the waist till I was looking at him from the space between my thighs.

"Like what you see?" I asked with an upside-down smirk. From this angle, I could make out the way his hardened length lifted the towel over his lap.

"Fuck, baby, yes, I do…" James replied, moving a hand in my direction. I stood upright and took a step back.

"No touching. You have to earn that," I said while looking at him over a shoulder. The struggle to restrain himself was apparent on his face, and the feeling of being so desired made me bolder. "Take off the towel. Let me see how hard you are for me, baby." I dropped the end of the belt from one hand and gripped my ass, spreading it slightly before turning to face him again.

He shifted the ends of the towel to the sides, his large cock erect and free.

"Hmm, you're so hard for me… I bet you'd love to stick that in me… here." Using my empty hand, I slowly traced my mouth. Sliding a fingertip down and tugging at my lower lip along the way. I continued to graze a hand over my neck, between my breasts, and down over my exposed core. His eyes followed my movements with the focus of a starved predator watching its prey. "Or here?" I glided a finger over my wet slit, moaning softly as I hook two more inside myself.

His right hand moved towards his cock, and I raised the belt and lightly dropped the length of it onto his lap.

"No, you don't get to touch yourself either. I'm in charge. You only get pleasure when I say so." I slowly removed my fingers from myself, brought them up to my mouth, and ran my tongue from base to tip before sealing my lips around the tops. Sucking them clean. "So sweet, just like honey. Would you like a taste, baby?" I asked before moving my hand back down and slipping my fingers inside me once more.

"Fuck yes, I need it," James growled.

"What's the magic word?"

"Please," he answered.

"That's a good boy. Open your mouth, stick out your tongue, and stay still," I instructed, and he eagerly obeyed.

I pulled my hand back and climbed onto the bench so that I was on my knees. Straddling him but high enough that the tip of his length couldn't touch me, I slid my arousal-coated fingers past my lips. Once I'd collected it all, I drew them out again and gripped James's hair, keeping his head tilted back as I spit into his waiting mouth. He remained still, just like I told him.

Leaning closer, I brushed my lips against his ear. "Swallow," I whispered before giving his lobe a playful tug with my teeth.

James's jaw snapped shut, his moan a deep rumbling thunder in his throat.

"Hmm, such a good boy you are." I kissed his neck, then stood and took a step back. "Now… lie on the bed. Strap your ankles into the restraints first and then one of your hands."

James pushed to his feet, and I couldn't help but glance down at his throbbing length as it bobbed in the air in front of him. Lying on the bed as he'd been instructed, he bound each of his ankles, then his right wrist. His eyes only leaving me once per restraint. I could see his jaw ticking, as if the notion of not being able to pin me down and fuck me right now was ripping him apart.

I stepped up and grabbed his free wrist, guiding it to the last restraint while ensuring I'd secured him properly. Then I moved around to the other straps, adjusting them until they functioned for someone of his height. I did have to tighten one of the ankles slightly, but I was surprised that he hadn't left his right hand looser. He was listening so well. More impressive than that was the fact he was actually letting me be in control, even though I could tell he wasn't used to this. Which was fine, because neither was I.

I opened the nightstand drawer on his side of the bed and pulled out the silky black blindfold he'd used on me. "Lift your head," I ordered him, tying the material behind his head and ensuring his eyes were completely covered. "You're going to be my fuck toy now…" I reached out and lightly stroked his hardened length with my fingertips. "You have such a nice cock. Maybe if you're lucky, I'll play with it. But first…"

Smiling, I climbed onto the bed and positioned myself so that my knees were on each side of his head, my feet resting in the pockets of his shoulders.

"Fuck, baby, you smell so sweet," he moaned.

I sank my teeth into my lip at the compliment but cocked my hand back and slapped his torso, causing him to hiss. "You speak only when spoken to. Your mouth's only purpose right now is pleasing me. Understood?"

"Yes," he bit out.

"That's *yes, Mistress*," I corrected, gripping his throat this time. I couldn't even come close to choking him, digging my fingernails into his skin instead. "Say it."

"Yes, Mistress," he answered just above a whisper.

"Good boy. Now keep your mouth shut until I tell you otherwise." I released his throat and placed my hands on the top rail of the bedhead.

Lowering myself, I sat my exposed core on his mouth. The warmth of his lips on me was a self-inflicted tease I wouldn't be able to endure for long. Letting some of my body weight press down on him, I began to grind against his face. The stimulation had my already-wet center igniting as I felt my arousal beginning to soak his beard against my skin.

I closed my eyes, arched my back slightly, and removed one hand from the rail to reach back and grab his length, my fingertips just barely meeting around his girth. He pulsed in my grip, his hips moving up like he was trying to fuck my palm.

"Eat my pussy and make me come, James," I commanded with a moan.

He didn't hesitate, and before I could take my next breath, his tongue was unhinged. Placing both hands back on the rail, I continued grinding against his mouth. Even in this position, this man knew exactly what to do. He worked his tongue on my clit, occasionally closing his lips on my heat to swallow and then resuming the same perfect rhythm. Most women might get frustrated by the brief pauses, but I couldn't complain. As wet as I was right now, he would likely drown if he didn't drink me in.

My heart was pounding in my chest, my breaths growing shorter and quicker as that familiar buildup rose to the surface. Just as I had the faintest inclination to warn him, the thought was erased by the pleasure.

On impulse, I reached down and gripped his hair as my thighs tightened around his face. And I erupted with hot, wet pleasure, each burst causing my body to seize until I was nearly falling forward.

18

JAMES

Warm, wet, sweet, and violent. My mouth was suddenly filled with the purest of passion as my girl convulsed, her pleasure erupting out of her, and I swallowed it all each time without thought.

New kink? No, addiction unlocked.

As her body began to relax from the shock of the orgasm, she raised slightly, allowing me a better opportunity to breathe. Not that I wanted it. I could die a happy man with my face buried between these thighs.

Let her be my headstone so I was always beneath her like this.

"Fuck…" she gasped, her hand reaching down to touch the spot beside my head. "Oh my god… it's practically dry…"

I lightly licked at her, careful not to overstimulate her after such a strong orgasm. "I would never let such sweetness go to waste," I said, softly kissing her wet lips.

"Fuck, you are such a good boy. I think it's time I reward you." The words escaped her in gasping breaths as she continued to recover. She moved down on the bed till she was straddling my hips, pressing my cock to my stomach as she sat her slit against it while sliding back and forth. "Is this what you want, baby?" She leaned down, the lace of her teddy brushing against my chest and her breath bristling the side of my throat, somehow stealing the air from my lungs.

"Yes, Mistress," I responded, fighting the urge to free myself and take her now.

I liked this side of my harpy, though. She was coming out of her shell more and more every day. I knew almost everything about her past, the good and the bad and the ugly. The strength and courage she was displaying by taking charge like this tonight turned me on to no end.

At some point while I'd been lost in my thoughts, she'd reached down and slipped the tip of my length inside herself. The warm sensation grabbed my soul by the throat, and we both let out a low breath as she slid down my shaft till she reached the hilt.

"You feel so good, throbbing and hard inside me," she said in broken moans as she began a slow up and down motion.

I gritted my teeth. She was right. She felt *so fucking good*, but I needed more. I couldn't resist any longer. As she continued to grind on my cock, I crept my hands up to the restraints, untying each strap from the bed. And then I let loose.

My palms shot to her hips, and she let out a shocked gasp. "Oh my god!"

I pinned her down on top of me and began thrusting up, fucking her from below. She grabbed the sides of my face and swiftly pushed the blindfold up. Our eyes met, locking on to each other as I continued to fuck her.

"Yes, James! Such a good boy! Fuck, don't stop!" she cried out.

Don't stop? As if that were even an option.

There was no stopping. I was already on the verge of coming, and I was going to fill my girl with every drop of my seed. "Fuuuuuck," I growled out as I gripped her tighter. Thrusted faster. Fucked her harder.

When I felt her begin to tremble, letting out the prettiest moan I've ever fucking heard, I erupted inside her with a force that I was certain was record-breaking. She collapsed on top of me, panting hard. Her arms framing my head against the bed as mine wrapped tightly around her torso. Both of us laid there for a moment, trying to recover from what had just happened.

"You ass… You could have gotten free that entire time?" she said, a light laugh buried between the hard breaths.

"'Course not. They just happened to get loose." I chuckled. Moving one hand up to the back of her head, I gently petted her before craning my neck to the side so I could press my lips to her temple. "I think we both need a rinse," I whispered.

Sera propped herself up on her arms and ran her fingers over my still-wet beard. "That sounds like a good idea."

Her eyes scanned over my face as her thumb traced my lower lip. The way the candlelight flickered making her pupils sparkle. The flames dancing, hypnotizing me in their magic, and silencing the storm outside.

And suddenly I was back home. Sitting on the hood of my dad's old Chevy in the middle of one of the pastures, on a warm summer night, watching the fireflies twirl over the tall grass. There was the remainder of a six-pack of Bud in a cooler beside me, 90s country music playing from a boombox off a burnt CD I'd made in high school. It was the most peaceful memory I had, the same one I'd escape to when things got bad overseas and I was too scared to sleep and needed to calm my mind. It was like my brain was overwriting that file, or maybe stitching this one onto it.

"I love you." *That was the second time I'd said it now.*

"And I love you, James." Sera smiled, kissing my lips before jumping off the bed. Totally oblivious to the near out-of-body experience I'd just had. Shaking my head and laughing softly at myself, I got up and grabbed my towel from the bench.

A short while later, we were showered, dried, and wrapped up in blankets, Sera's head resting on my chest.

"James?" she said softly, the familiar sound of fatigue in her voice.

"Hm?" I responded, my mind half in a haze as I gently stroked the top of her head.

"Are you sure you love me? I mean, it's not just me, you know. Alex and I are a package deal. Can you see yourself being a dad?" she asked as she traced the tattoos on my chest with a fingertip.

I kissed the top of her head before looking up at the ceiling. "I can. I might not have met him yet, but I love him too because he's a part of you. Besides, he seems like a pretty cool kid from what I've seen of him."

"Would you want more?" she said with a long yawn.

"Perhaps one or two. Though that's not just my decision. I'd be happy as long as I have you." I kissed the top of her head again and awaited a response. But none came.

Sera's breathing was soft and slow, a telling sign that she'd fallen asleep. Reaching out and picking up the candle on my nightstand, I blew it out and settled in as comfortably as I could without disturbing her.

On a typical night, I'd lie awake for hours, trying to hide from the demons that lurked in my dreams. Tonight, though, with Sera in my arms as I counted the rise and fall of her chest, it wasn't long before I too slipped off to sleep.

19

LOLA

"*F*uck me..." I placed the back of my hand to my pounding head and groaned, using the other to push myself up into a sitting position.

I could feel a mattress beneath me. *Beneath that*, the ground and not the couch I was meant to be sleeping on. Opening my eyes, I glanced around the room and instantly regretted the quick head turns when my vision blurred. My arm gave out from behind me and I fell backwards, landing on my side. I buried my face in my palms and took slow breaths, waiting for the spinning to stop. I tried to focus on the sound of the light rain outside and snoring somewhere nearby.

Great. My hangover was starting and I was still a little drunk.

Once the room started to settle around me, I lifted my head and opened my eyes. I had no real recollection of how the night had ended. I remembered starting the game, someone getting scared, James going to check outside...

Oh my God, I'd started fucking myself in front of James! But what the fuck happened after that?

It was then that a hand reached out and gripped my hip, pulling me back into something hard and warm. Pressing against my bare ass.

Oh, fuck, that's right! I'd ended up fucking James in front of everyone. But what about Sera? Wait...

I sat up in a panic. Looking back over a shoulder to the man whose cock was on my ass right now.

Oh, fuck no!

I felt my stomach twist as my eyes fell on Brian's face, last night's festivities returning to my memory. Something I knew I'd never be lucky enough to forget again for as long as I lived.

I'd drunkenly began fucking myself, displaying it all for James, and he'd silently rejected me. I remembered trying to take more shots, but Brian stopped me. That was until I'd talked him into taking a body shot of tequila from between my tits. After that, he'd taken two more, and I was pretty sure the second and third time, he'd licked the salt from my nipples.

Danielle and Jade had passed out on one couch or the other, leaving the two of us totally unsupervised.

Brian never really did it for me. The golden retriever kind of boy was the one you settled down and had babies with. He was not the exciting, live life on the edge and fuck on a Harley while flying down the road at 80 mph kind of guy. That was Mustang.

Regardless of all that, and with the alcohol in my system probably double what he'd downed, I'd decided it was a good idea to just fuck Brian and pretend he was James.

It hadn't lasted long or more specifically, *he hadn't*. I recalled being surprisingly impressed with his dick, though.

Reaching behind my back, I closed my hand around his dick. It certainly was impressive. He definitely had a few things going for him. Stroking my thumb over his tip, I continued trying to remember how I'd come to be naked in bed with Brian. My eyes drifted to the ground beside the mattress, to where a mostly empty bottle of tequila stood. A monument to a fun night.

Yep, that was it.

Brian and I had fallen back onto the mattress with the bottle and a bag of chips. Next thing I knew, he'd poured tequila on the head of his cock as I sucked it off his balls. That was pretty fucking hot, but I had no recollection of whose idea that was.

Then I remembered climbing up and riding him with his back against the couch. Danielle had been literally only a foot from my face as I'd bounced on Brian's cock. It felt fucking amazing at the time, being right up against Danielle as she slept somehow making it even sexier. But just when I was getting close to reaching my orgasm, I'd realized something was wrong. His cock had gone soft. The motherfucker had started snoring, and despite me dripping on his cock with my tits in his face, he'd fallen asleep.

I'd tried shaking him, gotten off his lap and started sucking his cock. I even put my fingers in his ass, for fuck's sake! But the fucker was out cold. I'd tried finishing myself off but the frustration and embarrassment had totally killed the mood for me. Eventually, I must have passed out and he'd scooted back down.

Maybe now he'd stay hard enough for me to get off.

Still lying on my side, I raised my outside leg while collecting a pool of what saliva I could muster onto my tongue.

Damn cottonmouth.

I licked my finger, then lubed myself up before reaching behind my back to help guide the sleepyhead's big cock right into my pussy. I slowly started to grind against him, fucking myself with his cock while reaching down and rubbing small, slow circles against my clit. I closed my eyes and imagined James behind me. Fucking me hard.

No, not James, *Mustang*. That fucking beast of a man. James was fucking hot, but his persona was the fuel for my best orgasms. It was Mustang's cock inside me right now. That insanely-imposing mask in the mirror in my mind as he took me from behind. Our eyes meeting as I became his whore.

Just a minute or two in—along with the combination of his cock, my fingers, and my fantasy—and I was already about to come so hard. That was until I heard, "Ah, my Lola," in that knockoff Henry Cavill voice that I had to admit was sexy.

But nice voice or not, my Mustang fantasy was shattered. I felt soft hands grip my hip, the lack of a rhythm throwing my own off. My frustration took over as I grabbed his wrist, squeezing it tight while urging him not to try doing anything more than he was.

I could totally still salvage this. Just needed to picture Mustang bending me over and fucking me till my soul left my body. Mustang fucking breeding me.

As if reading my mind and just as I began to think I might finally get off, I felt Mr. Bean shoot his load inside me. "Ah, that was so good… Lola, love," he moaned out slowly. "Wasn't it?" His words were still so slurred.

Fucking lightweight.

I tried desperately to thrust backwards and get myself to climax but it was useless. Like hitting a light switch, he was off. Cock soft and mouth snoring over my shoulder.

More frustrated than I'd ever been in my life, I got up, almost losing my footing and falling over him. Once I found my balance, I contemplated kicking him in the dick with all the force required to turn his amazing cock into a smashed hot dog. But that would be a waste. Maybe he could be trained one day. So, instead, I thought of something way better.

Fueled by the lingering tequila in my system, frustration, and the embarrassment of this fuck not only falling asleep while inside me but later having the audacity to come before I did, I stepped back till I was standing over his waist. With one hand extended towards him, middle finger up, I relieved myself on him. The wet sound louder in my ears than I'd thought it'd be.

My eyes flicked over to Danielle and then to Jade, but both were sound asleep.

Lucky bitches could sleep through anything.

A moan caught my attention, and my glare bounced around until it found the source. Beneath me, Brian (who was still asleep somehow) was lying on his back, his eyes shut as he reached beneath the blanket. Likely gripping himself.

Mr. Bean, you do have some taboo kinks after all. Bet you'd let me peg you.

Maybe I could salvage this poor man, given enough time. But who had that kind of patience?

Sighing, I looked around the room till I spotted my oversized *Callsign: Mustang* hoodie draped over the back of one of the couches.

"Oh, fuck yes."

Stepping over, I pulled the hoodie over my naked body, the hem resting a few inches beneath my ass as my hands slipped into the front pocket, instantly closing around three pre-rolled joints and my lighter.

"Salvation."

I stepped towards the front door, carefully cracking it open to check the weather outside. To my delight, it was merely misting and the storm had passed. However, in the dim moonlight, I could see how muddy it was out there. The only pair of shoes I had within reach were my old Vans. I couldn't resist the urge to slip my feet into James's cowboy boots. They were nearly double my size but they were certainly waterproof. Then I shuffled out the front door as quietly as I could, not wishing to wake up any of the others and risk having to share my weed.

Popping one of the small canisters open, I pulled the blunt out before I'd even made it down the front steps. By the time I reached James's truck, I'd already had it lit and was finishing my first long inhale. I dropped the tailgate of his truck, jumped on top, and finished blunt number one.

After blunt number two, I was feeling good again. 'Least good enough to go back inside and sleep. Slipping off the edge of the tailgate, I dropped my hands into my pocket, ensuring I had my last blunt and lighter. But as soon as my feet hit the ground, my eyes caught on a dark figure looking at me from the tree line, the promise of sunlight making the sky grey behind him.

I narrowed my glare at the tall, intimidating, blurry figure—*no, not blurry, that was the weed*—as it began to approach me.

"Oh my God," I whispered aloud when I recognized the half-skull mask with the red slash over the opposite eye.

Fear ignited in my mind, but the inferno that was already burning in my core seemed to fuel my entire existence. With my hands resting on the edge of the tailgate, I clenched my thighs together, knowing I was holding Brian's cum inside me. And suddenly, I was feeling more forgiving. I was way too dehydrated to properly get wet for my fantasy man. But Brian's cum? That would be the perfect lube, and Mustang would think that I was incredibly wet for him. Then maybe he would wake up and pick me over that cunt Sera.

My masked man closed the distance between us in the blink of an eye—at least according to my current state of inebriation, he did. His large, gloved hand gripped the front of my throat as the other lifted the end of my hoodie, the one with literally a picture of his mask on it.

I was about to get fucked by Mustang while wearing his hoodie! Fucking hot!

I let out a strangled moan beneath the pressure of his hand on my throat. "Oh, you want to be fucked?" he said in a deep but not gravelly voice. Not like the one I'd had on repeat in all my sexual fantasies.

What a time to be cross-faded!

A chuckle echoed from beneath his mask, and he released me just long enough to remove one of his gloves and drop it on the tailgate behind us. Next thing I knew, the fingers of that same hand were deep inside me, working in a hook motion that felt good but… off. Instead of pulling up and palming my clit as his fingers fucked me, he was scissor-kicking them, which was more distracting than anything else.

Come on. There was no fucking way my ultimate fantasy man didn't know how to fuck a woman.

Before I had the chance to shake the doubt from my head, he drew his hand back and raised it to my face. But he didn't look at it. His eyes were on mine as he used his opposite hand to tilt his helmet-like mask back. Then he slid his fingers into his mouth. But not until after I got a glimpse of a thick glob of what was certainly Brian's cum on his skin. There was no warning him. I didn't have time to process what I was seeing as he cleaned Brian's cum off his hand.

"Hmm, a little saltier than I'd expected, but so fucking sweet," he said, again without the gravel I'd imagined.

"Oh, God…" It was all I could say in my shock at officially making Mustang a cuck without his knowledge.

I also had little time to dwell on it. Because with a grab of my arms and a twist of my body, I'd ended up bent over the tailgate with my masked dream man frantically pulling up the end of my hoodie to reveal my tattooed ass. His hands were all over me, slapping, gripping, pulling. Almost as if he were nervous as he lowered his pants and revealed his cock.

Feeling his tip brush against my warm, wet, *freshly-fucked* slit, I tensed in anticipation for what I was confident would be the largest, most-amazing cock of my life. The disappointing realization struck me when he parted my lips and slid his *much smaller than expected dick* into my aching core. It wasn't even a fair salute to the overly-sensitive sleepy cock I'd had inside me just a few moments ago. Let alone the monster cock I'd been fantasizing about for the better part of a year.

Mustang thrusted into me over and over with all of what I

was certain couldn't be more than five inches. Determined to make the best of my situation, though, I reached one hand between my legs and found my clit. He might have had a small cock, but he could maintain the same fast and intense rhythm I typically liked. As lacking as it was, I was at the very least getting fucked like a cheap whore. I closed my eyes, enjoying each thrust, the tailgate cold and wet as it pressed against my nipples.

I was going to fucking come all over Mustang's cock, tiny or not. Not only that, but I was also going to steal my fantasy man away from the pretty Kardashian bitch Sera and let him put a fucking baby in me.

For over a year, I'd been grinding with my bookish TikTok account. I would give honest reviews while dressed in sexy outfits. I'd spent so much time building up my following. Then, all of a sudden, *MorphineKiss* appeared.

She was hot, fit, and a tattoo artist as well as skilled with video edits. She'd post her masked content in a sports bra and booty shorts, and her followers grew like emo kids waiting outside a My Chemical Romance concert. As if I couldn't hate her enough, she stole Mustang's attention from me.

But not anymore. Because now he was here with me.

I moaned, throwing my hips against him. "Oh yes, Mustang, fuck me harder, Daddy! I bet my pussy is way tighter than that slut's." I smiled, biting my lip, only to have it cut through when a strong hand gripped my head. Pulling it back and slamming it against the tailgate.

"Shut the fuck up!" he growled out as blood poured down my face.

There it was. He was angry. I'd spoken without permission.

After that, I was a good girl as he pounded into me and I kept my eyes and bleeding mouth shut.

James—Mustang was fucking me. He picked me. I'd won!

I'd tried canceling Sera multiple times through others

without ever being caught. In the end, I had to settle with just getting her content restricted for one reason or the other by spam reporting her page.

"I'm so fucking close, Mustang!" I cried out as I continued rubbing my clit between his shallow thrusts. "Please don't—"

But it was too late. He was already coming inside me. His cock grew soft and he'd instantly stopped fucking me.

"What the fuck!" I screamed. "You tiny-dicked fuck, you couldn't even let me come!" Before my brain could process what was going on, I felt something cold spread from one side of my throat to the other. "Wha…?"

His hand cocked my head back, then violently slammed it forward against the tailgate again but much harder this time.

With a crack, one of my teeth broke apart and tumbled out. My eyes saw it. My mind comprehended each bounce of my broken tooth as it made its way across the tailgate. The rest of me, however, was too distracted by the sensation of something tearing along my throat.

I looked down at the image in front of me. My vision had worsened, but I could clearly make out the splashes of red against the chipped black metal beneath me. The weirdest thing was I was growing so sleepy. I was about to give Mustang a piece of my mind and make him eat me out till I got off. Now, though, all I wanted to do was sleep.

My hands reached slowly up towards my throat, and panic gripped me when I held my arms out to look at them. Covered in thick, red blood.

I wanted to scream. I felt like I had the ability. He hadn't cut deep enough to hit my windpipe, just severed an artery.

I could still survive this!

I opened my mouth but before I could even make a peep, a sharp, hard, piercing pain traveled just below my rib cage and then shot downward, followed by the wet sound of meat on a cutting board. My body was tugged back hard, and in that moment before things went dark, I saw what the source of the sound was.

Beneath me, partially on the tailgate but mostly on the ground, was a growing pool of red. Surrounding a fleshy hose-like object coming out of me. My vision went black, my last thought a dying whisper in my mind.

I never even got to come.

20

JAMES

Something clanked against the sliding glass door to the patio deck. My first thought was that perhaps it was my imagination, but then I heard it again. Something small and hard bouncing off the glass. Sera was still asleep on my chest. Neither of us had moved the entire night. Reaching over and picking up my phone from the nightstand, I checked the time. It read 0636 hours.

The sun would be coming up soon.

With great care, I slowly began to work my way out from under Sera, moving my pillow into my place so that she still had something to cradle her. Then I made my way over to the patio door, scanning left and right before opening it quietly and stepping outside. Doing a continuous 180 while searching for the source of the disturbance. Nothing seemed out of place as I moved closer to the railing, my vision shifting downward to where my truck was parked.

Something was off.

The first thing that caught my attention was the fact that my tailgate was down. *Ask anyone who knew me, and they'd tell you I'd never leave my tailgate down.* It was one of the things I just couldn't stand. Like the sound of people chewing or odd numbers on a volume display. My friends said it was a compulsion or that I was just plain crazy, but any three of those things really threw my mood.

To add to my frustratingly-growing suspicion that something terrible was going on was the pool of liquid on the tailgate that appeared to be dripping onto the ground. Thanks to the color of my truck and darkness outside at present, it was impossible to tell what it was, though.

Moving back inside, I pulled on a pair of black sweatpants from the floor and grabbed my oversize hoodie off the door hook and threw it on. I was about to step out the door when the hairs on the back of my neck stood on end. Or maybe it was my PTSD-fueled paranoia. Either way, I turned, slid my hands under the mattress, and grabbed the shotgun I'd hidden there when I first arrived.

I then pressed a finger on the action release and pulled the slide back just enough to see into the chamber. *Empty.* I knew it would be, but I always checked. Drawing a buckshot from the extra four rounds on the side of the weapon, I dropped it into the empty chamber with the palm of my hand and slid the action forward. Quietly but firmly enough to ensure I heard the click.

I took one last glance at Sera before stepping through the bedroom door, locking it from the inside. The moment that door shut behind me, it shut on James too.

I was Mustang again—the nickname my buddies gave me back in my unit.

We'd all been dumb kids when we first met, with fresh memories of cool callsigns strong in our minds. It was during our first night in country, while we were all sitting around the smoke pit on the FOB, that we decided to pick callsigns for our personal usage on the squad. It was nothing we'd ever use on the radios for fear of being hazed but a little brotherly morale booster for us.

PFC Johnson - Scarecrow

LCpl Sanders - Reaper

LCpl Hollister - Goliath

LCpl Smith - Mustang

Scarecrow and Goliath never returned home from that deployment. The former had been mowed down by enemy fire and the latter had stepped on an IED.

On the next tour, it was just Reaper and me, each of us Sergeants at the time in charge of our own separate squads. After that second deployment, we both took our honorable discharges, shared a beer, and boarded separate planes to never see each other again.

Until a year later, when I was standing in a state I'd never been to before, watching as the last of my best Marine Corps brothers was lowered into his grave. The simple white coffin pinned with the Sergeant chevron I'd punched into it a few minutes before. Beside me, a sea of other Marines from our old unit. The asshole had to have a closed casket 'cause he'd suck-started a shotgun.

Just like the one in my hands right now. Apparently, his wife had left him not long after he'd returned home.

I'd had no idea.

I'd contemplated selling this gun many times, but my therapist told me I needed to conquer my fears and the things that triggered my PTSD. Any shotgun in general had become one, not so much because he did it. But because the same demons that convinced him to pull the trigger whispered to me many times as well.

Moving down the stairs slowly, I kept the butt of the shotgun in the pocket of my shoulder and the barrel aimed at the ground. The last thing I wanted was to wake anyone up and have them find me creeping down the stairs with a shotgun. That wouldn't go over very well at all. So, as quietly as I could, I passed the living room and moved straight to the front door. I glanced over to where my boots should have been but didn't see them. I also didn't have time to run up and grab another pair. I'd have to go out barefoot.

I reached the front door, opening it enough for me to squeeze out before quickly shutting it behind me. I paused to scan the area outside the cabin and saw nothing of interest, aside from a large shadow beneath my truck. I raised the weapon in my arms, muzzle towards my back tire, as I made a wide sweep around to the rear of the vehicle.

That was when I saw it. A scene so gory it rivalled just about anything I'd witnessed in the Helmand Province. A woman's body had been mutilated. She lay there on her back with her stomach torn open. The gruesome gash was deep and jagged, the skin uneven with irregular edges along the gaping hole in her abdomen. From her ribs to her pelvis. Her organs sprawled out on the muddied ground, nature already taking its course on her decaying corpse.

Her intestines were pulled out of the chest cavity, looped around her neck and… *my mask!* They were then twisted under her arms, where they were hooked onto my trailer hitch. Blood was everywhere. On top of the lowered tailgate and all around her body, which was completely nude apart from *my boots* on her feet, alongside one of my brand's hoodies. Between that and the various tattoos I could make out on her skin, I knew easily who the poor soul was.

I also knew better than to disturb what was clearly a crime scene, but we were in the middle of nowhere, with no power and no cell service. That meant no emergency services. So I did what I had to do. Because if there were any clues that could identify the killer, I needed to find them. I sat my shotgun against the back tire and raised the tailgate for a better look. Unintentionally, this had me placing one of my hands in a splattering of what must have been the victim's blood.

Damn it…

Once the tailgate was secured in the upright position, I rubbed the blood from my hand onto the sleeve of the dead woman's hoodie. That's when I noticed something sitting on the rear bumper, just in front of the license plate. I instantly recognized it as Lyndsey's phone—it was hard to forget the hot-pink case covered in jewels.

My curiosity piqued, I picked up the phone and illuminated the screen, expecting it to be locked. To my surprise, it wasn't. With a swipe of my thumb, the screen opened up and I flinched at what I saw. A still shot of an axe breaking through what could only be the leg of a very-nude, very-restrained Lyndsey tied to a very-familiar boat lift. The blur of the photo led me to suspect that it was actually a screenshot of a video. Opening the photos app confirmed it. The killer had recorded Lyndsey's last moments.

"Fucking monster…" I grunted, tucking the phone into my hoodie pocket before placing my hands onto the sides of my mask, presently resting on the victim's head. I lifted it slowly, her intestines making a wet, squishy noise as the helmet-like mask slid over her face. "Fuck… I'm sorry, Lola."

Her face was frozen in a mix of shock and frustration. Parting my fingers, I ran them down over her eyes, closing them for the last time. That was when I noticed the blood on the side of her face, which likely meant she wasn't wearing it when she died. This in turn meant the killer had already been in my and Sera's room, despite the cameras I had hidden throughout the cabin. I'd originally assumed it was someone in the group playing a prank, like maybe painting my mask pink.

That was what I got for assuming anything.

As I brushed Lola's hair back, my glare drifted to the wound on the side of her head and the small numerals carved into her skin: *3/6.*

"Close with and destroy the enemy," I cursed under my breath, reciting the start of 3rd Battalion 6th Marine Regiment's mission. Time and space around me seemed to freeze, my mind racing over everything I knew.

Someone was out here. Someone who knew how to get in and out unseen. Someone who knew how to cover their tracks well, perhaps survive alone in the mountains and was familiar with—

That was as far as my thoughts got before something hard cracked me against my temple, and everything went black.

21

BRIAN

James collapsed like dead weight, falling forward and to the left beside Lola. I slowly lowered his shotgun in my hands and looked down at the mess in front of me.

I couldn't believe that worked. I'd only seen it done in films before!

When I'd woken up naked in bed, it took me a few minutes to recall last night's itinerary. Lola had totally begun to come on to me after rejecting me for so long. She'd even offered to let me do body shots off her, which was wild and also my first time! She had finally come around. We had amazing sex in the den on the mattress, despite the other ladies being present. I didn't remember achieving an orgasm that time exactly, but I was certain she'd climaxed not once but twice.

Fuck, did she actually tell me she'd be my girlfriend? Or was that a dream?

Then, earlier this morning—*how much earlier, I wasn't sure*—she'd woken me up for round two! To make things better, in the sleepy haze, I must have confessed one of my more-taboo fetishes. I couldn't recall when she'd done it, but based on how wet and warm I was, she'd clearly catered to my dark desires.

At this point, I was certain she'd likely realized I was all of her favorite book boyfriends rolled into one neat-and-proper package.

None of that mattered right now, though. Because she was dead. Beyond dead. *What the fuck had he done to my love?*

I looked over at the grotesque scene in front of me, took note of the smell of her decaying body and the maggots already feasting on her corpse, before I stepped off to the side and got sick. My stomach turned inside out in seconds. Fortunately, it was mostly alcohol rather than a full meal. The toxic grog erupted from my throat. Fireball, Budweiser, tequila, and who knew what else spilling all over the already-wet ground.

As I began my second round of emptying the keg that was my stomach, two different voices cried out in incoherent panic. When I looked towards the source, I spotted Jade attempting to hold Danielle up, her screams cutting through the chilled morning air and right into my soul.

"Oh my God, Brian! What the fuck happened?" Danielle's eyes darted from me to Lola, then to Mustang and back to me. I couldn't bear to look down at Lola right now. I needed to handle James.

"Ladies!" I snapped. "I need one of you to go get the red duffle bag from my room. It should be on my bed. Please hurry!" I spoke loud enough for them to hear me without losing my control.

"Brian, are they both dead? What did you do?" *This* came from Jade.

"I don't rightly know! I heard something at the front door and couldn't find Lola. I stepped out here and found James hovering over her… like this!" The tears were starting to leak from the cracks in my armor. "Go get the bag! Quick!"

I couldn't take my eyes off the unconscious man below me. My right hand clenched tightly around the shotgun, the barrel hanging directly above his chest.

"I should kill you for what you've done!" I bit out as I struggled to hold back my emotions. "You stole her from me!" My finger crept towards the trigger. "Sick fucking—"

"Brian, what the bloody hell is going on down there?" Sera yelled from the upper deck, pulling me from my dark thoughts.

"Stay up there, Sera! You don't want to see this!" I replied, briefly taking my eyes off James to glance up at her.

The expression on her face broke my heart but there was a lot of that going on at present. As my glare returned to James lying at my feet, I realized my entire body was trembling and my stomach was still twisted up. I was no soldier. I was nothing of the sort. I sold insurance for a living. Violence was something that appalled me, just as much as gore. Yet, here I was, standing over another man with a gun in my hands while the woman of my dreams lay dead beside him.

The sound of crying stole my attention, and I turned to find Danielle with my bag in her outstretched arm.

"Hold it for me," I said before setting the gun on top of the tailgate and unzipping the duffle bag.

She glanced inside as I shuffled around the contents. Multiple neatly wrapped bundles of Shibari rope all freshly buttered. I'd taken lessons for months leading up to this trip and had hoped to impress Lola. Now, I was about to use them on her killer instead.

A tear escaped from the corner of my eye as I pulled two bundles of black rope from the bag and a roll of black duct tape. "Danielle, I want you to take the gun and go inside. All of you girls need to stay in the living room," I told her without looking in her direction, and then I began to bind James's wrists and forearms together.

Second rope.

I was certain handcuffs would work better but I only had the fun mock kind with pretty soft insides. James certainly would have the real deal somewhere, but I needed to get him restrained before he woke up and could kill anyone else. So my newly-acquired Shibari skills were getting their debut like this.

After a few minutes, his wrists and forearms were bound as well as his ankles in a double-column knot, just in time for him to start stirring. I looked back over to the cabin, my eyes focusing on the steps.

Well, he wasn't likely going to stay unconscious much longer anyway.

Grabbing James by the rope tied around his ankles, I dragged his limp form to the stairs and up, his head cracking against each wooden step along the way.

"What the fuck!" he growled out, flailing his body and trying to rip out of my grip.

"Don't bother, mate!" I replied as I continued to drag him into the house and over to the large walk-in pantry.

"Brian, it's not what it looks like! You got to hear me out! There's someone out there!" he yelled, attempting to rock himself into a seated position.

I grabbed the roll of duct tape, pulled at the end, and held it to the side of his head as he struggled.

"Brian, you aren't fucking listening! Sera! Her hu—" was as much as he got out before I secured his mouth, his eyes burning into me while I undid his ankle binding and tied the ends around the base of the bolted-in pantry shelves.

I hesitated a moment before I stood and walked to the door. He sounded so serious, like he actually believed what he was saying.

Shaking my head, I turned back to watch him struggle. "We're going to get the constables out here as soon as possible. Until then, you will stay put."

I was about to shut the door when a mix of loud voices gave me pause. But before I could fully pivot to look, something hard collided with my side.

"Brian, what the fuck! Let him go!" Sera screamed.

I had to reach out and plant a hand against the nearby wall to prevent myself from falling over as she landed a solid tackle to my side. However, in the time it took me to regain my footing, she was inside the pantry, crying out to James while cradling his body.

"Sera, no!"

22

SERA

"James!" I screamed as I practically fell into the room and dove onto his body.

I had no idea if I was doing the right thing but I'd heard everything he'd said, and I believed in him. Lola was his friend too. He wouldn't have killed her! No one was thinking right, least of all Brian I was sure. The guy was in love with her.

James struggled in my arms, trying desperately to tell me something beneath the duct tape, but all I heard was mumbling.

"It's going to be okay," I said softly as my tears dropped onto his face.

Then I lowered my head to his chest and reached my hands around to his, slipping the item I'd taken from his nightstand into his fingers. I felt his body calm, likely recognizing the familiar weight and shape of his switchblade. The chances of me getting Brian to let James go was definitely outweighed by the likelihood of Brian's grief overcoming him and causing him to execute James before we had a chance to figure out what happened.

Even if James somehow did do it, I couldn't bear the thought of him being killed. He very well could be telling the truth. Perhaps there was some crazy cult in these mountains targeting young adults. It had been done in so many films; it could definitely be the case here.

"Sera! Get off him. He's a monster!" Brian yelled from behind me as he gripped both of my arms so firmly I was certain to bruise.

"Brian, you're hurting me! Let him go!" I shouted in harmony with the somehow louder and more primal scream James made from beneath his duct-taped mouth.

His features had become horrifying in a way that restarted my brain. Veins bulging through red skin as if they could tear through his restraints, his eyes so dark it was as if all the pigment was gone.

I continued to struggle to get out of Brian's hold, but his grip was firm as he lifted me up. Something kicked against the inside of my foot and forced me to separate my legs. James seemed to kip beneath me, the action followed by a crunching noise, and suddenly Brian was collapsing onto my back, screaming in pain directly into my ear. All three of us were now piled uncomfortably on top of one another, me on top of James and Brian flailing on my back.

With a quick heave, I sent him flopping off and he sat up, his hands gripping his knee, which seemed to bend backwards while his leg twisted off to the side. My jaw dropped at the realization. James had knocked my leg out of the way and kicked Brian's knee with so much force that he'd broken it.

Oh my God, what the fuck had I gotten myself into?

I couldn't help but glance back and forth between the two men repeatedly. James looked like a caged beast, like something not of this world. It scared me.

"Brian!" Danielle called out just as she and Jade filed into the room, making the space feel more confined. The girls went to help Brian up before Jade broke off, grabbing and tugging me away from James. This time, I didn't fight it.

After all, did I really know James well enough to confidently argue that he would have never killed Lola?

I couldn't say that I did.

A couple of hours later, and we'd all finally settled into the living room after going off in pairs to grab our phones and other comforts. The power was still out.

"Sera, I'm sorry but you have no idea what that man is truly capable of. None of us do." Brian winced as he spoke.

None of us had any medical training beyond CPR it seemed, but apparently Jade was confident that she'd seen enough war movies to know that he needed a splint to keep his leg from moving and risking the broken bones around his knee slicing an artery. Therefore, she'd taken the handles off the mop and broom she'd found in the closet and duct taped them along the outside of his thigh. No one protested.

"Look, I wasn't going to say anything, but there's something you ladies don't know about him. Robert didn't have a family emergency. James beat the bloody hell out of him." Brian paused, grimacing as he tried to adjust himself on the couch.

"What!" Jade and Danielle called out in unison.

I said nothing. I was speechless and only half listening, as my mind kept replaying the events of the entire vacation. We'd made so many lovely memories, but then they all kept getting chased away by the image of James's face in the pantry. So much pent-up emotion that scared me to my core. Rage and a feral, menacing intensity.

"It's true. He'd claimed that Robert had tried to drug Lyndsey. Roofies. When I came inside, James was on the verge of killing him. Ended up saying he was going to make Robert leave and instructed me to keep it a secret so as not to ruin the trip for you girls. At first, I believed him. Always thought James was on the up-and-up. Now, though…" Brian paused, his brows furrowing as he shuffled towards the shotgun propped up beside Danielle's chair.

"Now you're thinking James actually killed Robert," Jade said, and began to cry again. She'd had a crush on Robert. Frankly, she had a crush on *everyone*. But Robert seemed to be the only one to encourage her, which made it harder on the girl.

"Oh, Jade, darling, I'm sure Robert is totally fine. He was in the live chat, remember? He can't be dead!" Danielle said, as she leaned over to wrap an arm around her friend.

"Yes, that's true, isn't it? Surely he's alive. Forgive me. I'm just trying to take this all in still. What I do know is that man is not coming out of that pantry so long as I live. Or at the very least until the constable gets here," Brian said in the weakest attempt to sound confident and comforting I'd ever heard.

I pushed up and made my way towards the kitchen, only to have Brian immediately protest.

"Sera, don't you dare!" he yelled, and I turned in time to watch him attempt to get up from the couch and fail.

"Easy, Brian. I'm grabbing something for Jade from the kitchen."

Stepping over to the refrigerator, I opened the freezer door and grabbed a tub of Ben & Jerry's "Totally Nuts" ice cream. It was one of Jade's favorites. It looked delicious, but I was deathly allergic to nuts. Then, because I knew she was so obsessed with having us believe she was sticking to her diet, I grabbed one of her kombucha bottles before I made my way back to her with a dishcloth, a spoon, and the treats.

"Hey, Jade, it's kinda melted and runny but it's still cold. I know ice cream really calms my nerves." I offered her a smile, and Danielle gave me a nod as she pulled back with Jade's approval.

"Ah, well. Yes, I suppose, in such stressful times, it's justified, right?" She sat up and wiped the tears from her eyes before reaching out and accepting the dessert and drink.

I leaned in and kissed her forehead. "This is all going to get cleared up. The power will be back on before we know it and we can get the constables out here to…" My words trailed off.

What the fuck were we going to tell them?

Hey, that's our friend out there. Two of our other friends are unaccounted for, and my boyfriend is tied up in the closet because we think he did it?

Oh, my days.

Moving over to the sofa chair, I dropped down and curled into a ball, pulling my oversized Mustang hoodie over my knees and feet and disappearing inside it. My mind was going to overheat and explode at this rate. The gears were all turning way too fast. How did I end up in a far worse mess than the one I was hoping to escape?

I dug out my phone and pulled up a photo of me holding Alex in my lap at the zoo. I would give anything to be home, holding him right now.

"Thanks, Sera." Jade broke me out of my daydream. She had the tub of ice cream between her legs and the bottle of kombucha in one hand, her spoon in the other. "This really did the trick. I feel so calm right now. Almost happy even."

Her words were surprising and out of place, but one look at her face told me she wasn't lying. Jade was grinning from ear-to-ear, her voice light and sleepy. She must have been in a state of shock.

"I'm glad they brought you some comfort. Everything's going to be okay." I smiled back at her from my hoodie cocoon.

"Yeah, of course things will be!" Danielle affirmed. "Sorry

guys, but should we like, go cover Lola up? I mean, she's just lying out there… exposed."

"You're right. It's the decent thing to do. I'll just—*fuck all!*" Brian grunted while attempting to get up from the couch.

"Will you stop fucking moving!" Danielle scolded him. She stood and pulled a blanket off the mattress on the ground. "Sera will go with me. We'll be right back. We'll take *this* with us." She grabbed the shotgun and tossed the blanket in my direction.

"Right, of course. Be right back." Grasping the blanket in my hand, I followed Danielle outside and over to Lola's body.

It took everything in me not to get sick. Jade and Danielle had described what had been done to our friend, but there weren't words for how horrible this truly was.

"Try not to look. Let's just place the blanket out over her and get back," Danielle said, setting the shotgun against the truck tire and stepping around to the other side of Lola's body. The smell infiltrated my nose, the unpleasant odor of death nauseating me.

"Was she religious? Should we say something?" I asked as we stared down at the blanket-covered lump on the ground.

"I don't think she was, but it couldn't hurt, right?" Danielle stepped back to my side and took my hand in hers. "Dear Lord, please—"

A loud scream erupted from inside. "Girls! Help!" *Brian.*

Danielle dropped my hand, lunged for the shotgun, and sprinted towards the cabin with me following close behind her. The front door slammed against the wall as we entered.

Part of me expected to walk in and find James with that mad look in his eyes, beating Brian with his bare hands. What we saw instead was Brian on the floor, crawling towards Jade. Her skin turning a light shade of blue and her pupils like pinholes.

"What happened?" I yelled. "Jade!" Danielle and I rushed to her side.

"It sounds like she's choking!" Danielle screamed, and she wasn't wrong.

Jade's breathing was eerily slow, and she was making gurgling sounds. Danielle quickly jumped up onto the back of the couch, leaned down, and wrapped her arms around Jade's chest. Making a fist while attempting to give her the Heimlich maneuver.

"Jade! Stay awake, girl!" I patted her cheeks as I watched her eyes glaze over just before they shut completely.

"She's limp! Is she out?" Danielle asked, still furiously pumping at Jade's chest.

"Yes, she's out! Jade! Stay with us!" Brian yelled.

I reached for Jade's neck, placing two fingers over her carotid artery. Danielle paused and looked to me. Her eyes wide. I shook my head.

"She's gone." The words barely made it out of my mouth. Two people were dead. Two of *my friends* were dead. Jade's body twitched once as it surely purged itself. Then she was still.

"It was like she was choking." Danielle slowly pulled away to start wiping the tears from her eyes. "Maybe an allergic reaction?"

"She's been eating ice cream since we got here. No, it's more like she was poisoned." Brian punched the floor beneath him. "We need to get out of here. Go get help. Sera, do you know where James's keys are? We can untangle Lola from the truck and drive down the mountain." His eyes were focused and filled with determination.

I nodded once, stood, and ran upstairs to where I knew James liked to hang his keys. By the time I returned, they were both outside. Brian sprawled out in the tray of the truck, and Danielle using the blanket to remove Lola's corpse from the tow hitch as carefully as possible. I quickly dashed off to help her, gently lowering Lola to the ground and leaving her there beneath the blanket.

"Come on, ladies. We need to be quick about it," Brian called out, tapping his hand on the body of the truck.

"Sera, I'll drive. Get in," Danielle said.

I nodded and turned on my heel to run to the passenger side, my body colliding with Danielle's. The force knocking me back a step as my feet tripped on something squishy. "Fuck! Gross!" I pushed myself off the truck and circled back around.

I made it one step before Danielle grabbed my shoulders. "You're in America, Sera. Right side!" she shouted, giving me a small push in the opposite direction.

"Why can't you Americans drive like everyone else!" I hissed in frustration as I climbed into my seat, feeling very off balance.

With that, Danielle started the engine and we sped down the driveway. Towards what we hoped would be safety.

23

JAMES

The room was completely dark, save for the thin razor blade of light coming from below the door. I could hear most of what was happening on the other side. Jade was dead. From what I gathered, it'd happened rather suddenly. Perhaps an allergic reaction but most likely a drug overdose. That was my gut feeling.

This situation was totally fucked. I couldn't logically be mad at Brian. He'd seen me lay into Robert like a freight train and then found me standing over Lola like that. Her body had still been rather fresh too.

If only he had given me the chance to speak…

"Afghanistan."

The singular word escaped my lips at the same time an old anger rose in my chest. I took that anger and used it as fuel, enabling myself to slide the knife Sera had slipped me faster against the Shibari rope. I'd been at it for at least ten minutes, trying to cut through enough of the rope before the pieces finally fell to the floor and my arms were free.

I took a moment to stretch and flex my upper body as the

feeling returned, then started slicing away at the binding around my legs. I'd just moved on to the second segment of rope when I heard it. The sound of my custom exhaust roaring to life.

Fuck, my truck!

I considered screaming out but that would be pointless. No one could hear me and I needed to get free!

The moment my legs were loose, I wasted no time sprinting outside to the front porch. "Fuck," I cursed through gritted teeth.

They'd stolen my truck, likely to try to get help. All I could do was hope they made it. In the meantime, I needed to arm myself and find a vantage point. Unfortunately for me, the only two weapons I'd brought were in that same truck. My shotgun and the hidden Glock I kept in a secret compartment in the back seat.

Thank you, Chevrolet.

I needed to get upstairs and grab my gear, but curiosity got the better of me first. Stepping into the living room, I walked directly up to Jade's body on the couch, her skin tinged blue.

"Rest in peace."

I shook my head and turned, making my way upstairs to the main bedroom. I immediately went to the duffle bag situated in the closet, picking it up and dumping the contents out onto the bed. All my *Mustang* gear, apart from my mask.

I put on my combat gear, boots, trousers, body armor, and gloves, my mind wandering to the sandbox in a country I never should have left alive.

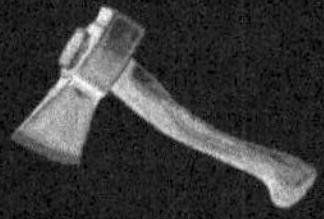

Marjah, Helmand Province, Afghanistan
15 February 2010

Day three of the operation and my squad had run into a British unit after almost taking each other out in the haze of battle. The enemy had launched a vicious counterattack, composed mostly of suicide bombers. The first two had been children we'd attempted to help out of the area. A sister and brother, both running towards us down the main street. We'd thought nothing of it and ushered them past us. My unit lost six Marines and a Navy Corpsman in that blast as well as two machine guns and our Gunnery Sergeant.

After taking the hit, we bunkered down in a large hut. The plan was to hold tight and allow other allied forces to push past us and then take up the rear as a supporting element.

A few hours into it, we noticed armed figures moving in from the west, working towards our position. In the chaos of battle, it was hard to say who opened fire on who first, but a brief gunfight erupted.

Thankfully, one of our Recon Marine Snipers had been watching us from elsewhere in the city. "Three-six-bravo! Blue on blue! Blue on blue. British friendlies to your west!" came across the radio.

Just like that, the gunfire went silent. And shortly after, we were sharing our hut with a British squad that had gotten separated from their main force.

"That's Reaper, Goliath, and I'm Mustang. How about you, part-ner?" I'd asked the British soldier, who'd sat down to play blackjack with us. The stakes? Cigarettes and candy from our MREs.

"Corporal Watson, Micheal Watson. You chaps can call me Mike." He had short blond hair and beady blue eyes that only a fool would trust. He had good stories and plenty of smokes, so we'd let him join in the game. After all, he was a new face and it was a chance to interact with our allies.

It wasn't long before Reaper and Goliath got called out to stand watch over the two most likely avenues of approach, leaving Mike and me alone in the hut.

"Blackjack," I announced for the tenth time as I set down a nine of hearts, a ten of clubs, and a two of spades.

"Fucking hell, I haven't beat you a single time. I'm done. Haven't got a cigarette to my name anymore. You've cleaned me," he cursed, throwing his hands in the air.

"Ah, don't worry about it, partner. Here," I said, handing him a full pack of Marlboro Reds from the stash in my assault pack. "America's best."

He picked it up and we spent the better half of the night chain smoking and telling stories about our time in country until the conversation shifted to stories about home instead. I told him things about growing up on a ranch, and he told me about the hundreds of women he'd had waiting for him—including his wife. His stories were accompanied by a handful of photos he produced from his wallet.

"This here is Amy. A beauty I met at uni. Here is Abigail. Oh, and Stacy." He continued shuffling the stack of Polaroids of half and fully naked women in his hands.

After girl number three, I'd honestly turned my mind off and was just politely nodding my head as this bastard bragged about how he was basically the biggest man-whore in his country. I was about to tell him to fuck off and try to get some sleep when one photograph caught my attention.

My hand shot out, my fingertip pressing on one picture he'd been about to breeze past. "Wait… Who is she?"

He paused, holding that particular photo out for me to see. It was of a raven-haired beauty. With the darkest, most enchanting obsidian eyes I'd ever seen. Her upper lip possessed this seductive cupid's bow and her body was decorated in very elegant, fine-line tattoos. Which peaked out of the black lace lingerie she was wearing.

"Oh, that's just Sera. My wife. Not by choice, mind you. Got her pregnant and, well, things are rather old-fashioned. You understand, right? What do you people call it? A shotgun wedding?" He laughed and sat the photos down on the ground between us as he lit another cigarette.

But I couldn't take my focus off the photo of the woman with the obsidian eyes.

I shook my head and realized that I was now holding a photo in my hand, brushing over it with my gloved thumb. The same photo I'd stolen from that British soldier back in 2010.

My harpy, my Sera.

The woman who'd unknowingly stumbled into my life. I opened the Velcro pouch of my body armor, slid the photo directly over my heart, and pressed the fabric back down. Before dropping two of my throwing axes into their holsters on my thighs, the other two gripped tightly in my gloved hands.

Unable to resist, I stepped into view of the closet's full-length mirror. "DC Comics, eat your heart out."

24

SERA

Sitting in the passenger seat of James's truck, all I could smell was him. The warm and comforting mix of cedar, tobacco, and pine. It had my thoughts jumping from demanding we go back and get him, to wanting to just get on the first plane for home.

A sudden bump in the road brought my mind back to the here and now, and the seemingly endless forest surrounding us.

"Wait, flashing lights! You see those red-and-blue flashes? Just up there, around this bend—*what the fuck?*" Danielle might as well have read my mind because that was exactly what I was going to say. The truck slowly came to a stop, and she put it in park as we stared blankly at the scene in front of us.

"Ladies, what's the trouble? Why have we stopped?" Brian called out to us, the sound of shuffling telling me he was turning around. "Oh, God."

"That's Robert's car… and the sheriff's truck. Oh, fuck! Is that…?" Danielle opened her door, and before I could protest, she was out and slowly walking towards the other two vehicles.

Not about to let her go anywhere without me, I threw open

my door and went after her. "Brian, stay here! We're just going to check it out!"

"Ladies! Be quick! And don't go too far!" I could hear the panic in his voice as he scrambled to push himself up, his makeshift splint banging against the metal.

We didn't get more than a few steps before we saw it. Just past where Robert clearly ran off the road and wrapped the front of his car around a tree was another body. A portly man in a well-kept uniform. Aside from the collar of the blouse, which was tinged red at the spot where his head should be. A large, similarly-colored stain covering the front of his truck, expanding outward from the winch situated on the grill.

My eyes scanned over the man's uniform. Evidently, Danielle was doing the same thing. Because, at the same time I noticed it, she gasped. "His gun is missing. Whoever did this for sure has the gun. Oh my god! We're going to die!"

She was on the verge of becoming hysterical. So I did what any friend would do. I grabbed her shoulder with one hand and slapped her right across the face with the other. "Snap out of it!"

Her eyes went wide and she froze. "Ouch…"

"Danielle, where is our gun?" I asked calmly.

She pulled out of my grip and sprinted back. I turned to follow her, but a thought occurred to me as soon as my eyes fell on our vehicle.

"We're blocked!" I spun towards the constable's truck, rushing to the driver's side and yanking the door open. "Damn it!" I cursed when I realized it was in fact *not* the driver's side again. Instead of wasting more time, I climbed up into the truck and crawled over. "Fuck!" I punched the steering wheel in front of me.

"What's wrong?" Danielle panted from behind me with the weapon now in her hands.

"The key's missing. We can't move it," I huffed.

"What about the radio? We can call for help!" she cried out in a tone that could have been mistaken for joy as she jumped in beside me. She grabbed a coiled cable hanging from a small box under the dashboard. "Fucking fuck! It's cut off!" She picked up a palm-sized microphone before tossing it over my head and into the woods.

"Ladies! Ladies! Run back! Now!" Brian's panicked screams had us hopping down from the constable's vehicle and looking back towards the truck, where he was struggling to stand while frantically gesturing behind us. "RUN!"

Bang! There was a deafening boom, followed by the shattering of glass as the headlight to Danielle's left erupted.

"Run, run, run!" Brian continued to scream as Danielle turned around and raised her weapon.

"Run, girl!" she shouted as she fired at something or someone beyond me.

Pain erupted in my shoulder and sliced through the top of my ear, throwing me off balance and causing me to spin to the ground.

"Fuck, Sera! Who the fuck puts buckshot in first! Fuck, girl!" Danielle cried out as I tried to process the growing warm, wet sensation dripping down the side of my neck.

"You fucking shot her! I thought you Americans were born with guns in your hands! Get her in the truck! He's coming!" Brian's screams were frantic and, at the moment, dizzying too.

"Sera! I'm so sorry, girl. Come on! I got you. Please hurry," Danielle said low under her breath as she heaved me up to my feet and draped my arm over her shoulder. Just as we took a staggering step, another bang sounded and the windshield spider-webbed out and shattered.

Danielle propelled me forward, the shotgun in her hand beating against me as I dared to look back. My eyes honing in on a tall figure standing a few yards away from the constable's truck. Dressed in all black, he appeared thin but muscular and he wore the standard Ghost-skull face mask over his entire head while above it rested a stonewashed bone crown. The tactical vest was decorated with an assortment of glow sticks over the belly, a Union Jack emblem on his sternum. It was all terrifyingly familiar. Yet the most alarming thing about him was the gun he had aimed in our direction.

Before he could take another shot, Danielle was shoving me into the truck. "Scoot over! Quick!"

I did as I was told, whimpering as my arm grazed the seat. I glanced over to Danielle just in time to see her raise the shotgun and fire.

"Is that KingArthur?" I gasped at the realization.

Callsign: KingArthur was a masktoker who'd been in and out of our group more times than I could keep count of at this point. One moment, he was saying something extremely outlandish in our Discord server about one of the women. More often than not, though, his focus was on me or attacking any of the men who responded to my photos in the NSFW section of the chat. Yet somehow, every time he got kicked from the server, the majority would bring him back in after some half-assed apology and threat of suicide.

When this trip was first being planned, he was meant to attend. He'd even contributed to the cost of the cabin for the week. Then, just a month prior to our arrival, he'd backed out. In an *@everyone* message, he'd stated that he was taking a break from social media for his mental health and wished us all the best.

A week or two later, he was practically forgotten about. Till now.

I got no reply. The booming thunder of the shotgun pierced my ears but offered comfort at the same time. Just as I raised my head to look through the shattered windshield, Danielle slammed the driver's side door shut and started the engine.

"Did you hit him?" I asked, easily spotting the panic in my own voice.

"I don't think so! But I think you're right! I think that was him!" she yelled out as a loud bang cut through the air and the rest of the windshield fell in on us.

"Reverse, ladies!" Brian screamed.

Danielle changed gears and slammed her foot down on the gas pedal, dirt and rocks kicking up around the truck as it raced backwards at a concerning speed. I glanced over to find Danielle peering over a shoulder while steering the vehicle and somehow keeping us on the road.

"How the fuck are you doing that?" I asked.

"I'm from the country. Grew up off-roading. Driving back-wards is second nature," she answered, but her tone told me I should stop distracting her.

So I focused on the space where the windshield was meant to be, my eyes widening when I saw the figure waving at us. *No, at me.* His glare was locked directly on me, and judging from the wrinkles in the corners of his eyes, I could tell he was smiling.

25

JAMES

I'd found my mask downstairs. Sitting on the kitchen counter still splattered with Lola's blood. I set the axes down and picked up the mask, my eyes locked on my trademark TikTok persona. It was just an airsoft mask I'd heavily modified until it looked like the face I'd seen in my nightmares since coming home. It wouldn't stop a bullet, but something about it in my hands just felt right.

Unable to resist, I put it on, reaching up and cinching the straps tight. I took one deep inhale and grabbed for my axes. When I let out the breath, it was like my body came alive. Someone was out there putting my harpy's life at risk. They were going to find out there was only room for one monster on this mountain.

Stepping out onto the front deck, I scanned the woods in front of me. My glare settling on the road. A vehicle was coming back this way. And fast. Judging from the sound of kicked-up gravel, I'd say it was my truck. Which meant they'd found something that they didn't like or couldn't get past. They were headed here, likely to take up the defensive and await emergency services.

Not a bad idea. They were using their heads.

Every fiber of my being screamed at me to run into the woods. It would only make sense for the killer to have a camp he used to observe the coming and goings of the group. I took off in a dead sprint, not caring for stealth. Whatever noise I was making would be hidden under the growing roar of my truck's exhaust and the gravel it tore up on the road.

The terrain beneath my feet wasn't too bad. Steep and rocky in places. But apart from that, I merely needed to jump over the occasional fallen branch. Off to the east, my beautiful blacked-out lifted Silverado flew backwards at a speed that made my gut twist. That sense of pain stabbed twice as hard when I noticed the windshield was missing and my headlight had been shattered.

Was Sera okay?

I caught myself turning to keep the truck in view, in hopes I'd see her beautiful face, but it was too far and moving too fast. Shaking my head, I brought myself back to the present. I couldn't get distracted right now.

The silver lining was that I had no doubt my target was ahead, and it seemed whoever was at the wheel was very capable. Turning my attention back to the woods, I sprinted up the next hill and dropped down between a cluster of jagged boulders and two pine trees. Then I cleared a spot by my feet, proned out, and waited for my target to come to me.

26

SERA

The figure grew smaller and smaller until it was gone altogether. At the speed Danielle was driving, it wasn't long before the cabin was back in view. In fact, we were practically there and she wasn't slowing down. If anything, she was speeding up. When I looked up to Danielle, her face was frozen, her eyes locked on to the rearview mirror. At first glance, I thought she was hyperfocused but I quickly realized she was in shock.

"Danielle!" I screamed at the same time Brian shouted something unintelligible from the back.

Danielle shook her head, coming out of her trance. "Oh, fuck, fuck, fuck!" She yanked the steering wheel to the side, nearly missing the light post in the front yard.

"No! Not that way!" Brian called out a little clearer, the truck jumping and rocking as it ran over something large.

The moment it was level again, Danielle slammed on the brakes, put the vehicle in park, dropped her forearms and head onto the steering wheel, and began to sob. "Fuck! What're we going to do, guys?"

The answer was: *I had no fucking clue.* But we couldn't sit in this truck and cry about it. We needed to let James loose. Surely the appearance of this other masked man while he was tied up in the closet would prove his innocence?

Reaching out a hand, I patted Danielle's back. "First thing's first, we need to get inside and get James out. He was in the military. I'm sure he can protect us."

Her only response was a nod of her head as she opened the truck door and stepped outside. Following her lead, I did the same, sprinting towards her when I heard her scream again.

"What?" I asked. But I didn't need her to answer me. My eyes landed on what had caused the truck to jump so abruptly. In front of the driver's rear tire was Lola's mostly-covered body. Her head now exposed and her face nearly unrecognizable.

Brian glanced down from the back of the truck and gagged. "Oh god, Lola!" He quickly turned away, bile spewing out of his mouth and onto the cab.

Snapping into action, I grabbed the blanket and recovered Lola's face. "Guys, there's nothing we can do for her anymore. She's gone. She's just a corpse now! But we aren't. We still have a chance. Danielle, help me get Brian down, then get the gun and let's get inside!"

Dropping the tailgate, I ushered Brian forward, and soon Danielle and I had him out of the truck and I was helping him up the stairs as best as I could with his arm slung over my shoulder. I could tell he was attempting to take on most of the weight with the way he was staggering.

The moment we stepped through the open front door, my eyes went to the pantry. *James would know what to do.*

Danielle and I helped Brian to the nearest couch, setting him down as gently as possible. "I'll get James. He can help us move Jade somewhere for now."

My shoulder was radiating with pain, but the bleeding wasn't too bad. Although I knew I'd need to clean it and bandage it up soon. First, though, I needed to get to James. Without even waiting for Danielle's response, I sprinted over to the pantry door and threw it open.

"James!" My heart fell.

He was gone, and all that was left was the rope that had bound him. I'd completely forgotten that I'd sneaked him the knife, and now I had to admit as much to my friends.

"Fuck! James, where are you?"

I took a deep breath and headed towards the living room, where the others were taking turns being hysterical and comforting each other. I couldn't bring myself to approach them just yet. Instead, I made my way back outside to James's truck. Stepping over Lola without looking down at her, I opened the back door and began to rummage through the interior.

I had no idea if I truly knew who James was anymore, but I was certain that a man *like him* would have a few survival items hidden around.

"There we are," I said out loud to myself when I pulled out a red medical bag from under the back seat. It was full of supplies I didn't know all the uses for.

I eagerly grabbed the gauze, a big bandage, and the medical tape. Digging a little deeper into the bag, I randomly grasped a small white bottle with the bold letters VA on the cap.

"Oxycodone. Yes, please." Returning the bag to the spot where I'd found it and shutting the door, I stepped back over Lola and headed inside.

"Where's James?" Brian questioned the moment I entered the room.

"He's gone," I said quickly, then tried to change the topic. "But look! I found some really good painkillers. Here, take one. It'll help." I attempted to open the bottle but the pain in my shoulder spiked, making me drop it.

Luckily, Danielle was there to pick it up and open it, dispensing a pill and placing it in Brian's palm before handing him the only drink in reach. A bottle of Fireball. "What do you mean *he's gone*, Sera?" she said in a broken voice.

Brian swallowed the pill, chasing it with three gulps of the cinnamon-flavored whiskey. Danielle snatched it from him and took just as many.

"Right, I tied him up perfectly. He couldn't have gotten loose," Brian added.

Danielle placed a pill into my waiting hand, and I popped it into my mouth before grabbing the whiskey and taking a quick shot.

"I may have sneaked him a knife when I ran in there earlier." I moved over to the sofa chair, carefully pulling my hoodie off till I was in just my black Sullen Art sports bra, and examined the wound. It really wasn't as bad as it felt.

"You did what? So he isn't innocent and that was him out there!" Brian yelled, and I flinched out of habit. Ever since Micheal, I couldn't bear to be yelled at.

Thankfully, Danielle came to my rescue. "Brian, there's no way that was him. He'd have to be the Flash to beat us out there in the truck," she said, but her tone told me she wasn't so sure either. "Sera, let me help you with that. I'm a vet tech back home. Not the same as a nurse, but I know how to work a bandage."

So much for none of us knowing more than CPR. Then again, I didn't know how much of a difference there was between animal patients and human patients.

It took Danielle a moment to walk over to the table of liquor and swipe up a bottle of vodka with a blank look on her face.

"What's that? Fuck!" I hissed as she pulled off the top and poured the alcohol onto my open wound.

"That's for setting James loose without telling either of us," she said coldly without even looking at me. Then she took the gauze and bandages from my lap and began working on my shoulder. "It was just a small buckshot pellet. When we escape this place, you'll have to have a doctor actually dig it out of you so you don't get an infection." She spoke softly while working some of the gauze into the hole in my shoulder with her finger.

It hurt but the pain killer was already starting to kick in. I raised the whiskey bottle to my mouth and took another shot. *A little more couldn't hurt?* I liked pain, but I think I'd found my line. Getting shot wasn't going to become a new fetish for me.

"Look, we don't know where James went. He could have run for help. There's a lake not far from here. He could be out there right now, trying to make it across to one of the other cabins and get us help," I stated, my eyes shifting towards the sliding glass doors, imagining that I could see him right now, shoulder-deep in the icy water, attempting to save us all.

Once Danielle was done patching me up, the two of us went around and checked that all the entrances were shut, locked, and covered. We'd all agreed that our best bet at this point was to bunker down and wait for help. Attempting to pass the time, we engaged in a spontaneous game of "fuck, marry, and kill" but after the twentieth round, we fell silent. Aside from the growling of our stomachs.

After we'd watched what happened to Jade when she ate the ice cream, none of us would dare consume anything, apart from the water straight from the tap, or the alcohol apparently. An hour later, Brian limped over to the table, scanning the bottles of liquor, appearing to decide that if death was upon us, he didn't wish to be coherent.

Danielle, on the other hand, was pacing the room. Shotgun in hand and eyes darting from the front door to where Jade still sat on the couch with a blanket over her, just like Lola.

I'd actually been about to dip off when the muffled sound of a distant gunshot broke the silence. Danielle rushed over to the window and peeked through the closed curtain, while Brian and I sat up and stared in her direction.

27

JAMES

It took much longer than I'd expected for the target to appear. More than an hour. Maybe two. My limbs had begun to fall asleep, and I had to quietly shake them out one at a time. Just as I considered going farther out to try to find his camp on my own, I heard the snapping of twigs. Someone was headed in this direction at a pace fairly fast for just an afternoon stroll.

Slowly moving backwards and closer to the trees at my side, I ensured I was well out of sight. And less than a hundred yards down the hill from me, out from a thick patch of pine trees, stepped a man. Dressed in all-black, tactical-style clothing much like my own. He looked to be just a few inches shy of six-feet tall, with a strong build but one that he'd let go a bit, and he was wearing the classic *Call of Duty* Ghost mask. But the mask itself wasn't what truly caught my attention. It was the stonewashed bone crown resting just above it.

Callsign: KingArthur.

The figure looked up to the hill where, unbeknownst to him, I was waiting for him like a rattler ready to strike. He bounded up the terrain, stretching his legs as far and fast as he could before landing himself about ten yards to my east.

I waited till he was in a comfortable range and then I leaped to my feet, my left hand cocking back and tossing one of my axes at his chest. His eyes doubled in size when he spotted me standing to my full height, and I committed the look of fear in them to memory. By the time he turned to reach for something at his waist, it was too late. The axe struck high and to the right, just on top of the rib cage.

"Fuck!" a male voice yelled out in a familiar British accent.

After that, everything seemed to speed up. He spun on the impact, one of his fists gripping the handle and pulling the blade out as he hit the ground. I kept two fingers on the second axe I'd holstered on my thigh as I moved to a better vantage point to launch my next attack. Then, dashing behind a few trees so that I stood directly above my Ghost-faced enemy, I reached a hand down, preparing for the next blow. Until my glare landed on the .357 Magnum duty revolver he'd unexpectedly drawn and aimed in my direction. The same one some sheriffs in Texas still clung to, despite most departments switching to the more modern Glocks or SIGs.

I didn't hear the shot. The moment my eyes zeroed in on the shine of the barrel, I threw myself to the ground, without knowing if I'd been hit or not. The next thing I heard was the loud crunching of boots on fallen twigs and pine needles. I rolled to the side, stopping on my chest and launching myself forward, tackling the man just as he broke the top of the hill, the gun flying out of his grip.

We rolled down the hill in a tangle of limbs, kicking and punching. The scent of pine and wet earth filled my nostrils and mixed with the strong salty stench of unwashed sweat. We were each getting pretty solid blows in.

A knee to my outer thigh sent pain shooting up my leg. I landed a right hook, but he gave me an uppercut that had the air leaving my lungs. Unfortunately for him, I didn't give a fuck about fighting fair. We rolled to a stop at the base of the hill, and he straddled me, attempting to wrap his hands around my throat.

The Hollywood choke. The Marine Corps' mixed martial arts program was viewed as a joke by most. But in truth, if you practiced the techniques with focus and an open mind, you could become a force to be reckoned with.

Slipping my arms between his, I bent it at the same time I bucked my hips and pushed at his opposite shoulder. Suddenly, I was straddling him. He moved his arms in front of his face without hugging his head. This man had some degree of training. As I aimed jab after jab at his face, he blocked while rocking his hips, attempting to throw me off my balance, much like I'd done to him.

Realizing his plan was to exhaust my energy, I threw the occasional jab at the axe wound on his chest. By the second jab, my fists were dripping with his blood. The color was like a drug, the purest hue of red. All I wanted in that moment was more. More bloodshed.

"How dare you interrupt my plans! You should have stayed across the pond, partner!" My voice was deep and filled with a primal rage.

Despite the barrage of punches, he sneaked in a blow to my side, throwing off the rhythm I was trying to maintain and giving himself an opportunity to speak.

"Oh, what's the matter, mate? Afraid I'm going to take that pretty little whore from you? Sera was never yours to begin with. I know what you've done!" He coughed and hissed through the pain.

At the mention of her name, I'd blacked out and reached to my thigh where my last axe still rested. Before I could pull it out, however, he'd managed to buck me off. Crawling away and gaining enough distance to safely get to his feet. The world suddenly shifted as something hard slammed against my head, likely his boot. Then my body collided with the ground.

Every attempt to stand was betrayed by my glitching senses. My equilibrium had been rocked by the blow to my head, making my vision seem to blur. It was also growing hard to breathe through my nose, which was stuffed with something warm and wet. Judging by the strong scent of copper now mixing with the fresh pine, I assumed it was my own blood. The only thing I could trust was my hearing. I could hear the sound of breaking pine needles and wet earth growing farther away from me.

I staggered to my feet, my gloved palm landing on the smoothly-polished handles of one of my throwing axes. Gripping it tightly, I turned to look up the hill, at the back of the man at the top of it.

"Watson!" I yelled at the same time his body began to turn. Everything seemed to slow down now, like a slide show presentation from the 1990s.

My hand cocked back as he raised the revolver before I even released the axe. I watched the round leave the barrel and tensed my body in anticipation. By the time the second round was in the air, aimed right at me, my axe had only made it halfway to him. Meanwhile, I felt the punch of the first shot to my chest, taking the air from my lungs. The next one hit me a fraction of a second later. The world moved, but my body was no longer responding to my thoughts. My back hit the wet, cold ground with a booming *thud* and my head rocked in my mask as it bounced off something hard beneath me.

Trees. Sky and trees. That was all I could see now. Blurry trees and a gray sky.

"Don't worry. I'm going to take such good care of our girl just like I did that Lola bitch. No one will recognize Sera when I'm done with her," he called down, mocking me.

I could barely comprehend the words, but the name... Her

name. *That* was all I needed to hear to understand he was threatening my girl. Despite how badly I wanted to spawn some sort of superpower and falcon-punch the fuck out of this bastard, he had the gun and the higher ground.

Mom said those Star Wars movies would rot my brain.

Knowing my best chance to save Sera was to play dead so I could regroup and catch him off guard, I remained as still as I could. Until I heard the snapping of a twig off in the distance, in the direction I'd last seen KingArthur. I waited a little longer before I slowly raised my head, my eyes locked on to the barrel of the gun aimed down at me, but there was nothing I could do but embrace it.

"Goodbye, Mustang." His words were drowned out by the sound of the third and final shot to my chest.

Fuck, that one might have gone through, I thought to myself before I couldn't think anything else. Because my world had gone dark.

28

SERA

We'd heard a total of three more gunshots, and none of us were sure how we felt about it. My first hopeful thought was that James had somehow found a gun and hunted down the masked killer. I knew better than to be too optimistic, though. Plus, it had been almost an hour since we'd heard anything. The two most likely cases were that law enforcement had arrived to save us or the killer had found James and now he really was dead.

I stood, walked over to the kitchen sink, and splashed cold water onto my face. "Fucking hell…"

Danielle had resumed her pacing around the outer perimeter of the living room. Meanwhile, Brian had fallen asleep on the couch and was currently snoring loud enough to have the killer thinking we had a pet grizzly bear in the cabin with us. The truth was, I much preferred the sound of him sleeping over the snide remarks casting blame on me, him crying over Lola, or stating how much he had to live for.

Like, mate, no one's life was worth that amount of tears, I thought to myself, not wishing to actually kick him while he was down. *The UK was in danger if Brian here was the new standard of man.*

Breaking away from her patrol around the living space, Danielle joined me beside the sink. She pulled a glass down from the cupboard and rinsed it multiple times before filling it with water. We were all still paranoid about ingesting whatever may have killed Jade.

"You okay?" she asked without even looking at me.

I nodded slowly, forcing my gaze towards her. "Yeah. I'm sure those shots were the authorities squaring off with that masked man. They'll be knocking on the front door to tell us we're safe anytime now," I said as confidently as I could.

"I don't know, Sera. It's already starting to get dark out. It'll be pitch black again soon, and there still isn't any power." Danielle shook her head but there wasn't any panic or sorrow in her voice. Just defeat.

I took a step towards her, leaned in, and wrapped my arms around her shoulders. "We are going to be perfectly fine, Danielle. Help is coming."

She nodded in reply and patted me on the back. Our faces slowly rising until we were looking into each other's eyes. Hers a brilliant burst of color and mine dark like night. There was no camera in existence that could tell you who closed the distance first. Her or me. But somehow our lips collided, fueled by more than half the seven deadly sins: lust, greed, gluttony, and wrath.

I barely registered the sound of the heavy shotgun being dropped on the kitchen counter beside us as my hands tore at her clothes. Her hoodie now on the floor, exposing the petite and perky peaks of her breasts. Instinctively, my palms drew up to them before I gripped her under her arms and lifted her onto the worktop.

Taken by desire, I lustfully yanked down the lululemon leggings she wore. I didn't know what was driving me at the time. All I did know was that our lives were up on the Grim

Reaper's chopping block, and I was going to make the most of it. Once her leggings were on the ground, I turned back to her, positioning myself between her open thighs. Our lips met again as she helped me out of my own hoodie and shirt, only pausing to work the material over my head. And then I was on her again.

I tugged at her lip with my teeth, placing one hand on the back of her head to prevent her from pulling away while my free hand was busy exploring her body. Appreciating every curve and the perfect fit of her breast in my palm. Needing to know how nicely her perky nipples would fit between my teeth, I fisted her hair and pulled it back hard. Taking my time as I kissed and bit down her jaw and over her neck.

As I went lower, she began running her nails up and down my back. She was being gentle with me, when I needed to be reminded that I was still alive. I bit her nipple. She shrunk back as far as she could till my hand hit the cabinet behind her.

"Ouch!"

"If you're going to use your nails, you better leave marks," I said, staring into her eyes. Seeing how desperate she was for this moment between us.

My tongue poked out and I ran the tip over her nipple in small circles, causing it to harden into a peak under my sensual touch. Turning my attention to her breasts, I hummed with plea-sure as Danielle clawed at my back.

She reached down, caressing the side of my breast before moving to pinch at my pierced nipples. Her other hand contin-uing to claw at me as I took two fingers into my mouth, running my tongue over the tips and getting them properly lubricated before gliding them between her thighs. She was so warm and wet with arousal that there'd been no need for me to add anything.

I stepped closer till my thighs pressed against the worktop, my lips brushing over hers, but I didn't close my eyes. Instead, I watched her lashes flutter as I slid my fingers inside her. Hooking them up. Slow but firm. Then my tongue dove into her mouth, her hand still on my breast, pinching my nipple hard. I responded by increasing the speed of my movements. Her arousal pooling on my palm and slowly running down between my fingers before catching on the worktop. Tinging the air with her sweet scent.

I needed to taste her.

Withdrawing my fingers, I gave her lip one last bite before grabbing her at the shoulder and opposite hip and pushing so that she was sitting, one foot up on the worktop as the other draped over the front. She shoved the toaster and air fryer to the side and tucked a dish towel under her elbow for comfort, accidentally knocking over a tall cylinder filled with spatulas, spoons, and other utensils. They clattered out and we froze, our eyes going wide as if we'd totally forgotten where we were, or that Brian was sleeping in the other room. Neither of us moved a muscle. My hands on her knees with my tits out, and her completely naked apart from her socks.

Then we heard it. Brian's snoring. I could feel the moment both of us relaxed, letting out all the tension we'd been holding in, and started to laugh. I stared intently into Danielle's eyes— every bit as beautiful as the photos in the hidden folder of my iPhone.

More so.

There were a few weeks before Mustang came into my life that I seriously considered giving up on men and just fucking women. Danielle was exactly my type too. Petite, with a nice ass, freckles, and a *girl next door* demeanor. And our flirting in the early days told me that she had a tiny freaky side just waiting to be nurtured.

I felt a brief moment of guilt at the realization I was being unfaithful. The truth was, though, James and I had talked about my bisexual curiosity and fantasies. I'd been so nervous when

I'd first brought it up to him. Micheal would have raged, called me *sick* and a *whore*. His brand of degradation was not the sort I got off on.

To my surprise and relief, James supported me, without the usual: *Oh my God, so I can fuck another chick?* He listened. He let me share my fantasies of being alone with a woman and was especially delighted that some of those fantasies included pleasing him too. I'd even told Danielle about the fantasies I'd had about the three of us on this trip together.

No, James wouldn't have a problem with this one bit.

The lower I got, the wider her thighs spread for me. Her pussy glistening with her arousal. My mouth sealed over her, my tongue like an insatiable beast. Resting one arm under her leg, I gripped my breast with my free hand. My thong warm and wet with my own arousal. After pinching my pierced nipple, my fingers then slipped below the waistband of my sweatpants and right into my hot, needy core. My inner walls tightly gripped my fingers as I worked them in small, hooking motions, occasionally pulling them out to rub at my clit before slipping them back inside again.

The faster I fucked myself, the more fiercely I licked and sucked at Danielle's clit. Her legs flexing till they were shaking. She was about to come for me like a good girl, and I wasn't going to let her pull away when she did it. With some reluctance, I drew my dripping fingers from between my thighs and slid them inside Danielle. Just beneath my tongue. My other arm wrapping around her raised thigh as I leaned into her, making it clear she wasn't going anywhere.

"Oh fuck, Sera! Please, I'm coming." She let out a muffled cry that turned into a high-pitched squeal. Danielle was a screamer, and right now, I couldn't care less if Brian woke up.

I continued to lick her up, washing my face in her arousal. Her hand combed through my hair, then gripped it tight as her body continued to tremble.

"Oh my fuck…" she said, panting as I took a few final licks, collecting her honey on my lips.

"You taste so sweet," I purred before kissing her, letting her taste her own arousal. "But now it's my turn to have my kitty licked."

She smiled and carefully slid off the worktop. "Hmm, yes, please, MorphineKiss." She giggled as she turned us so we were swapping places.

Then she kissed me again as she slid her fingers beneath my sweatpants and directly inside me. The suddenness caught me off guard, and I gasped.

"God, you slut. You're so wet," she said as I started to hump her hand, eager for my own release and the idea of a woman going down on me for the first time.

"Errghm." The loud sound of a male clearing his throat from the other room had us both freezing and looking that way.

"What happened to—" I began.

"The snoring?" Danielle finished.

"Um, ladies. If you could please cut your girl time short and join us. I mean *me*. In the living room, please?" I recognized the same grief in Brian's voice that had been there before he'd fallen asleep. But there was something else there too now.

Fear.

Danielle and I slowly separated. She rushed to pull her clothes back on, tossing me my hoodie while she was at it. Then she grabbed for the shotgun, raising it as we stepped towards the opening that would give us a straight look into the living room.

We spotted Brian's feet dangling from the end of the couch as we entered. Two more steps, and he was fully in view. And so was KingArthur. Still in the Ghost mask as he stood behind the couch. He had Brian's hair gripped in one fist while the other held the end of a gun to the poor guy's head.

"Um, ladies, help, please…" It looked like Brian was about to say something else, but before he got the chance, our masked intruder tapped the barrel against his temple.

"If you ladies could be so kind as to step out from behind there, please. Oh, and only one hand on the shotgun, Ms. Danielle. Thank you," the figure said in a distinctly English, very polite voice.

Too polite really. So polite it was condescending more than anything else. Everything about it was familiar. The thing was, none of us had ever heard Arthur speak before. He'd always typed or used his tablet during lives.

"Fuck Brian. Just shoot him," I whispered under my breath, my lack of empathy for my friend surprising me. Something about our Ghost friend was so terrifyingly familiar that it made me want to scream and lash out.

Danielle glared at me in disgust and took the lead, stepping forward with one hand in the air, the other aiming the shotgun towards the floor. Without much choice, I followed her out into the living room, my eyes never leaving the masked man.

"That's good enough, ladies. Thank you. Mrs. Watson, why don't you sit right there beside your deceased friend?" He pointed the barrel of the revolver at me, then gestured over to the empty space next to Jade. "Shame about her, really. I'd planned her end so well, you know. Looks like something didn't quite agree with her," he said as he leaned towards Brian, speaking to him as if they were long-time friends. "There's Daddy's Sera Doll," he added as I settled myself onto the couch, and my hands instantly gripped the cushions beneath me.

"There's Daddy's Sera Doll! Daddy is home and so horny." The words from my nightmare—from my *reality*—haunted me.

I couldn't move. He'd found me. I didn't know how, but he had. The only people who knew about my trip to the United States were my parents and my best friend Kearsten. The three of them and the Discord group. That was it.

Wait! Fuck, Sera, it's right in front of you! Focus! Micheal is King-

Arthur. My brain wasn't able to keep up with the information pouring into it all at once.

My eyes locked on to the masked man, but I couldn't speak. I felt like a deer in headlights. Every one of my senses was in a panicked state. My body wouldn't respond, my audio and visual senses having slowed down. It was like some nightmare version of *The Matrix*, only I wasn't Keanu Reeves.

"And you, my pet... You come over here and help Mr. Brian to his feet. No crazy ideas. Slowly hold that shotgun out to me, barrel down." He took a step back from Brian while ushering Danielle forward.

I wanted to scream, run, attack, *anything*. But I couldn't. The fear had me frozen in place, a prisoner to my past trauma.

29

DANIELLE

Frozen in place, the shotgun death-gripped in my hand, I was self-aware enough to admit that there was nothing I wanted more than to shoot him in the dick. Sera had been right. It was *Callsign: KingArthur.*

This asshole had been a pain in my ass ever since he'd joined our Discord server. I'd never figured out for certain what his beef with me was, but I'd always suspected it was my relationship with Sera. Anytime she and I openly flirted in the chat, he'd found a way to try to shift attention onto himself. Then, when she and I had calmed down and her relationship with Mustang kicked up, he got even worse.

At one point, he'd started using photos of a tall, fit, tattooed man, mostly shirtless with a Call of Duty mask on. While most of the group believed they weren't actually his pictures, the majority of us didn't care enough to call him out. Accepting that he likely had major issues with his confidence and image, and that this was his escape. A way for him to feel better about himself. And with us being an empathetic community, we didn't want to ruin it for him.

He was supposed to come on this trip, and all of us were surprised and curious to see what he really looked like, but he'd canceled not long before everything was finalized.

Guess he decided to come anyway.

I did as he ordered, not wishing to have Brian's blood on my hands or get shot myself. "Here, Arthur, take it. Just be cool. You don't want to kill anyone. We're friends, remember?"

His icy-blue eyes bore into me, chilling my entire being.

"You're hurt," I stated quietly, noticing the dark crimson leaking from his chest and another cut on the top of his shoulder. "I can help bandage you up. I can—"

He slowly raised the barrel of the revolver to my gut and pushed lightly, shutting me up without further argument.

"Exactly. Arthur, no need for any more violence, right? This is just some crazy joke, isn't it?" Brian said, attempting to force a chuckle, but it was clear he was on the verge of crying. His confidence likely drowned out by the alcohol.

Arthur's hand closed around the action of the shotgun, and I slowly pulled my arm away.

"Thank you. Now please help Mr. Brian up, and the two of you stand in front of the fireplace." He took a few steps back, tucking the revolver into his waistband and raising the shotgun towards us.

I kept my hands where he could see them and carefully helped Brian to his feet.

"You all won't mind if I enjoy some of your liquor will you?" Arthur said, stepping over to the table with the alcohol while never taking his eyes off us.

"No, of course not. Help yourself, Arthur. There's plenty. We could all just sit down and catch up with a few?" I said, trying to sound as pleasant as possible.

I glanced around the room as I helped Brian over to the fireplace, my eyes landing on Sera. She was totally bottled up, the euphoria that the two of us had shared in the kitchen minutes ago a distant memory.

The sound of a drink being poured brought my attention back to Arthur. "Oh, a wine guy, huh? Always figured you for a whiskey guy for some reason," I said in a light, teasing tone as I tried to figure a way out of our current situation.

"Danielle, could you be so kind as to shut the fuck up?" Arthur looked over to me, and I could have sworn he was smiling from beneath the mask. Keeping his eyes on me, he walked over to Sera, resting the shotgun up against his shoulder with one hand while clutching two glasses of red wine in the other. "Here you go, my dear. For what is a show without a nice drink?"

When she didn't move or even look at him, he let out a disappointed sigh and sat both glasses down on the end table beside Jade's body on the couch. He quickly ripped the blanket off her. Revealing the pale, stiff corpse of our friend.

"Oh, Jade, you've looked better, my dear. Would you mind holding Sera's wine for her?" He paused a moment before picking up one of the glasses and setting it between her thighs. "Thank you so much, my dear." He patted her dead cheek, and the mere idea of him violating her body by simply touching her face had me fuming.

But I was powerless. Standing next to the fireplace as Brian rested one arm along the mantle to keep his balance.

"What show, Arthur?" I dared to ask.

He didn't answer right away. Instead, he grabbed the second glass of wine and stepped back over to the sofa chair, where he could see all three of us.

Where he could shoot us, if he wanted to.

"You and Brian are going to put on a sex show for Sera and me. She always wanted to spice things up in the bedroom, try new things. I admit I never humored her. So we're going to watch some live porn right now." He raised his glass in the direction of Sera, as if to offer her a toast.

"You can't be serious. I'm not even into men." I looked from one person in the room to another before refocusing on Arthur.

"That is quite all right. I remember you saying you were a drama kid in your younger days. Just act it out." He smiled as he got comfortable on the chair, setting his wine on the stand beside him, but I didn't miss the way he winced when he did it.

There was going to be an opportunity for us to overpower him. There were three of us, after all, and he was wounded. I looked from Sera to Brian again, taking in their physical and mental states.

We still had him outnumbered even if all of us weren't in the best shape at the moment.

"Look, Arthur, she and I don't need to do—"

BANG! Brian's attempt at helping the situation was cut off by a thunderous gunshot and a splintering of wood.

"Fuck!" I screamed while Brian and Sera appeared to react in a very similar way.

Arthur was leaning forward in his chair, the shotgun now aimed at Brian, after having added a new hole in the wall to the side of the fireplace. "That's enough talking. No more talking! Danielle, be a good girl and get on your knees for Brian," he commanded, and I obeyed.

My body trembled, and my ears were ringing as I slowly dropped to one knee and then the other in front of Brian. When I looked up at him, I realized he was shaking as much as I was.

Our eyes locked, and he whispered, "I'm sorry."

I let out a steadying breath. "It's okay. We're friends. We'll be okay."

"What did I say!" Arthur barked out, waving the end of the shotgun at us as if we could possibly forget we were at gunpoint. "Now pull his cock out and give it a good suck for us. Sera, make sure to watch, my dear." He racked the action of the shotgun, ejecting the spent shell to chamber the next one.

That was when it occurred to me…

How many shots was that? One, three, four? Definitely four. Meaning there were more than likely four or five rounds left.

Assuming James put one in the empty chamber when he added a full tube. So, all we needed to do was hope Arthur was dumb enough to give us at least five more warning shots. Then we could all attack him at once before he was able to draw the revolver.

Maybe one of us could live. Or maybe not.

My scheming was cut short by something warm and soft tapping my forehead. "See that, mate? She's hypnotized by your cock. Good, smack her with that beast," I heard Arthur say.

He was right. I'd totally zoned out, trying to think of a plan, and hadn't realized Brian's dick was hanging in front of my face.

My god.

We'd all joked about the man likely being hung like a horse based solely on how square he was. This, though, this extra limb in front of me was as close to a dream come true as possible for any monster smut girl. I held back a smile, imagining the viral videos of booktokers reacting to the *couldn't fit two hands around it* sound clip.

"Let's go, Danielle. Get to work!" Our captor punctuated his command with another shot. This time aimed above the fireplace, the shrapnel of the stone raining down on us as we shrank into ourselves and covered our faces.

Four more. Maybe three.

There was hope we were going to survive this. Reaching up, I wrapped my palm around Brian's cock, and even flaccid, it was more than a handful.

I didn't even like dick, but I could appreciate this one. What was Lola thinking?

Curious to see how big this monster truly was, I looked up at

Brian, locking eyes with him. He was handsome. I'd give him that. Nothing compared to Sera, though. So I closed my eyes and thought about how amazing her tongue felt on my clit.

I tried my best to mimic the passion and skill she'd used to bring me to orgasm and put that to work on Brian's cock. I'd only ever sucked one dick before, and it wasn't horrible. And right now, it was strangely sexy. I was truly fucked in the head, because if I was being honest with myself, even having this psycho aiming a gun at us—forcing us to do this—was turning me on.

Taboo, taboo, taboo! I heard one of my favorite Booktok influencers saying in her high-energy Speedy Gonzales sort of way.

He was growing so fast in my mouth. I could feel the thickness of his length fighting against my jaw, forcing me to open wider. I slid my head back, popped him out and reached up, putting one hand over the other. Twisting and stroking him as I worked my jaw. Trying to prepare myself. I glanced out of the corner of my eye. Sera was still seated on the couch, but it appeared as though she'd picked up the glass of wine from Jade's lap and was now just staring at it.

Meanwhile, Arthur had his cock out and was rubbing it between an ungloved thumb and finger. His dick looked like a hairless baby mouse compared to what I held in my hands.

Seriously, if anyone was King Arthur, it was Brian. Because this was the Excalibur of dicks.

We were going to survive. Patience was key. After we made it through this, maybe I'd spend a little more time with Brian here. Patience.

30

BRIAN

Never in my life had I had a woman do what Danielle was doing to me right now. I'd gotten the occasional blow job, naturally, but I wasn't exactly a guy who got around. More so, I lived through the books I read.

In real life, I never really thought of myself as much of a man. My father had viewed me as a disappointment because I hadn't joined the army like he and my brother had. Then, after my younger sister had enlisted in the Navy, that had been really it for me. I'd been practically disowned.

I wasn't brave, didn't know how to shoot, wasn't very strong... And, honestly, at twenty-five years old, I was still afraid of the dark.

Even in the fucked-up situation I'd found myself in, Danielle was somehow making me feel like a man. The things her tongue was doing to my cock were blowing my mind. I struggled to maintain my balance, holding on to the fireplace mantle to keep myself upright. Danielle drew her head back and spat on my cock before sealing her lips around the tip and using both hands to stroke my length. My entire body shuddered and my legs grew weak, causing me to grab the mantle with my outside arm now.

It was then that my left hand collided with something else. The large clock that sat in the center. Made of dense wood, the kind they used in the early 1900s. That was when an idea came to mind. Waiting for the opportune moment where Arthur was completely entranced with our display, I would toss the clock in his direction. Catching him totally off guard so that I could lunge forward, grab the shotgun and become the hero! I'd prove my father wrong and perhaps even get the girl in the end.

"No! You cannot come until I'm ready!" Arthur barked at us.

Looking over, I realized he had his dick out and was clearly trying to get hard. I watched as he spat into his hand and began stroking himself.

This could be our opportunity. If he was frustrated, focusing on getting hard, perhaps he would be distracted enough for us to try something.

I glanced back down at Danielle and gave her a smile through the moans escaping my lips. Holding up five fingers and tapping my wrist, I then closed that hand into a fist and acted as if I were throwing something before gesturing a mock explosion. Trying to relay the message that, in five seconds, I was going to toss the clock at Arthur. And after that, we'd attack.

Her eyes went wide, and she nodded in understanding. She must have been impressed, because she started sucking me harder and faster, quickly bringing me to the next level of euphoria. I began my internal countdown, my body tensing and relaxing as Danielle brought me closer to climax.

One.

Carefully, the fingers of my left hand inched closer and closer to the mantle.

Two.

My hands closed around the top of the clock as Danielle

shifted one of her palms from my shaft to my balls. She was taking me deeper and deeper into her throat. I could hardly focus.

Three.

I lifted the clock into the air, my body shaking. I couldn't hold it back any longer. Danielle's grip on my cock tightened, and I began to erupt into the back of her throat. My hand with the clock going numb to the point I almost dropped it.

"What the fuck!" Arthur screamed out.

Then there was a loud noise. Suddenly, my face was warm and wet, and I was in excruciating pain. My legs gave out, and the room was spinning as I fell backwards, my head cracking against the fireplace.

My eyes sealed tight as I waited for the room to still. I opened them and glanced down to where I could still feel the weight of Danielle's body against me, followed by the growing sensation of thick, warm liquid.

When my vision cleared, my brain couldn't process what it was seeing. My body was unresponsive. Instead of Danielle, my gaze landed on a mess of what could barely be recognized as a human head. The upper half was gone, all but a few patches of hair and teeth, through which I could see what looked like raw ground turkey in her mouth where my dick should be. As if it couldn't be worse, my right hip was practically nonexistent.

At that moment of realization, I screamed. I couldn't hear myself screaming, but I could feel my throat going raw. I was screaming louder than I ever had, because what else could I do?

My eyes drifted around the room, as my hands instinctively reached for my groin, until I spotted Arthur hitting the chair with a fist as his other hand struggled to work himself back into his pants. My gaze then shifted to where Sera had been sitting. And wasn't anymore.

I was going to die alone. I knew that. The last thing I could do with my life was scream, in hopes I'd keep this psycho's attention a little longer and allow Sera to escape.

My world started to blur, my body going numb from blood loss. I didn't even register that Arthur had closed the distance till he was standing over me, the shotgun suspended between us. Then he brought the stock down. Hard.

I got one last scream out. Then that was it.

31

SERA

Up until I heard the first gunshot, I'd been mentally lost. Trying to determine if this was actually happening. It was impossible to wrap my head around. Not only had *Callsign: KingArthur* been my ex-husband this entire time—seeing my conversations and spicy photos in the Discord server—but now he was here! How had I left myself so vulnerable? How had I not been more careful? It was my fault that all my friends were dead. And James…

Oh my God, James must have been dead too.

I needed a drink, for no other reason than I wanted to feel something. To remind the rest of my body that I was still alive. Looking slowly over to where Arthur had placed the wine between Jade's thighs, I reluctantly reached for it, careful not to touch her.

Then, glancing from Arthur to where Danielle and Brian were positioned by the fireplace, I took a sip of the wine. It was dry and rich with elements of oak and dark berries and an undertone of vanilla. In this moment, it was so good that I took another sip, trying to focus on each specific ingredient. I wasn't a frequent drinker, but right then, I needed something to calm my nerves and slow my rapidly beating heart.

The room was quiet, apart from the wet sounds of Danielle sucking Brian's cock at gunpoint and the *dry* sound of Arthur's hand repeatedly brushing against the lap of his pants. He wasn't hard. Danielle was incredibly hot and worked Brian's dick better than I'd ever seen it done before. And yet, Arthur—or should I say *Mike*—was softer than a limp noodle. And by the looks of him, the only thing growing was his frustration.

There had to be a way to sneak away. Maybe catch him off guard? What I really wanted to do was smash this glass against his face. That was not an option, though. At least not a smart one, given the present fucked-up circumstances.

First and foremost, I was confident that the man beneath KingArthur's mask was somehow the boogeyman I'd married, my abuser, the one I'd fought so hard to escape. Secondly, that same boogeyman had two guns at his disposal. One of which was aimed at my last two living friends, assuming Lyndsey wasn't alive. After seeing Robert's car, I was pretty certain she wasn't. Then I had to take into account that I was in the middle of nowhere, in a strange country, without any signal. It was dark out, and to top it off, I'd already been shot once today.

I looked around the room slowly, trying to formulate a plan. One that would hopefully end with my ex dead and the three of us alive.

"What the fuck!" Micheal screamed out from where he sat, and by the time I glanced back towards the fireplace, all I could do was watch as one of my best friends in the world was literally blown away.

Self-preservation took over, my fight-or-flight instincts activated, as I dropped the wine glass onto the couch and took off without looking back. I was out of the room before my friend's body even hit the floor.

I dashed to the base of the stairs that led up to the main room. The expected sound of heavy footsteps didn't follow me.

He hadn't noticed my absence yet.

I crept up the stairs, praying to any great being listening that these wooden steps wouldn't give me away. I'd made it to the halfway point when I heard a loud scream followed by repeated banging. The third impact sounded wet, and I knew what was likely happening. There was nothing I could do to stop it either. So I continued along the stairs and over to the bedroom, holding my hand tight over my mouth while trying not to think about Danielle or Brian.

I slipped inside the room and locked the door, then rushed to where James's luggage was stowed in the closet. Pulling out his suitcase first, I rummaged through the contents, praying for a machine gun, a flamethrower, maybe a tank…

I found none of the above.

"What the fuck, James! What kind of American are you? I thought you all had like twenty guns at all times." I pushed the suitcase to the side, pulled out his duffle bag, and dumped it on the floor, instantly regretting it.

Whips, ball gags, handcuffs, candle sticks, ropes, some metal-spiked wheel thing, and at least five differently sized metal butt plugs. And still no gun.

Throwing the bag to the side, I stood and searched the room again. Desperate. Praying to find some secret hidey hole where James might have stashed one of the many guns he'd joke about having. I tossed one of the lamps from the nearest nightstand onto the bed and dragged the piece of furniture over to the tall vintage wardrobe in the corner. Climbing up so that I was just barely able to see over the top.

"Fucking nothing," I cursed under my breath.

From the other side of the bedroom door, I could hear the heavy footsteps ascending the stairs. That's when I noticed something hanging on the back of the door. Beside one of my jackets and one of James's branded bill caps was my keychain clipped to my coffin-shaped purse.

Normally I was a basic girl. I didn't often rock name-brand clothes outside of InkAddict, Sullen Art, and Calvin Klein underwear. When it came to accessories, I enjoyed the typical alt-girl style bracelets, chokers, rings, barbells and so on. And what was presently dangling from my keychain was a blindingly-pink, bedazzled, palm-sized cylinder. Something so unlike me. Because I hadn't bought it for myself.

I rushed over to unhook it from my keychain, turning the cylinder over in my hand. "James," I said aloud, choking on the threat of tears.

He'd always given me shit for not having my own form of self-defense. The thought of me going out while not being able to carry a gun frustrated him, and he kept saying it was time I moved to America. Little did he know that I typically had at least two knives on me ever since I took my son and left. I'd even joined the occasional boxing class at my local gym. This woman was far from the defenseless girl Micheal had married.

The moment the footsteps stopped, so did my heart. "Oh, Sera Doll, Sera Doll, let me in," he called out while softly knocking on the door. "Or I'll have to huff and puff…"

The rest of his twisted nursery rhyme died off, as I focused on the sound of metal being slowly dragged down the door. He was fucking with me, trying to scare me, put me on edge so he could control me like he used to.

Not fucking happening!

I adjusted the pink canister in one hand and reached for the door with the other. My fingers carefully pinching the lock and slowly turning it as he continued tapping the metal on the frame and violently shaking the handle.

I closed my eyes and tried to focus on the rhythm of his banging. I had to time this just right—otherwise I was certain I'd be dead. A half a second following the bang of metal on wood, I yanked the door open, extended the canister in front of me at his eye level, and pressed down on the trigger button so hard I thought my finger might break under the pressure. At the same time, I screamed. Not out of fear, but a fucking harpy's war cry. As if my scream alone could rip the flesh from his body and leave him a gory sack of blood, bones, and rotting organs.

"Fuck! Bitch!" Micheal cursed as his hands shot up to his face, the grip of the shotgun still clutched in his palm.

The barrel tipped up over his shoulder, and he must have tensed while reaching for his eyes because the shotgun went off right beside his head. The kick rocked his arm backwards at an unnatural angle as the side of the gun cracked against his skull, and then he and the shotgun both tumbled down the stairs. I watched, both astonished and delighted that my simple tactic had provided such pleasant results.

Micheal cursed and groaned, his body stopping when he reached the bottom.

He had to be dead.

I watched for any sign of life, which didn't take long. He groaned, trying to collect his limbs. And like a domino effect, his movement spurred me back into action. I ran over to the lamp on the bed, picked up the cable, and yanked it out of where it was still plugged into the wall. I glanced down at the intricate design, a mess of deer antlers stacked into a tower-like structure, all supported by a lightbulb at the top. It also had a weight to it that made it both beautiful *and deadly.*

I aimed at Micheal's head and threw that lamp down the stairs with every ounce of my strength. It was a direct hit. He went limp. I couldn't say how long I stood there before I took the first step down the stairs, down to where the body of my boogeyman lay. The body of the man who was supposed to be my best friend, my forever, and the father of my child.

One, two, three. Each step was a descent and ascension at the same time as I grew closer and closer to conquering my personal devil.

I shifted myself towards the wall by the staircase and carefully crept over him. My eyes darting to the shotgun at his side. The back end stained red with small chunks of pink wet flesh. But all the layers of thick black clothes he was wearing made it difficult to tell for certain if he was dead or unconscious. I stared down at his mask and closed eyes and dared to hope for the former.

Leaning over to observe him more closely, I tapped him twice with my foot. Nothing. Not even the twitch of an eye.

"Finally dead, are you? I wish you had been a better person. Alex at least deserved to have a good dad," I muttered, unsure of what to call the mix of swirling emotions consuming me.

Then I grabbed the base of his mask from around his neck and began to pull it up. Slowly revealing the weak jawline and cleft chin I could draw with my eyes closed. When the mask finally cleared his face and the familiar scars I'd given him across his eyes, I let out the breath I didn't realize I was holding.

Micheal.

I had no idea if I'd said his name out loud or in my mind. The world seemed to be spinning as I threw his mask across the room, keeping my eyes locked on the spineless excuse for a man who'd been haunting me with the mere knowledge of his existence. There were so many nights I went to sleep wondering if I'd wake up while wishing I wouldn't because I didn't know what I would be waking up to.

Would I wake to my husband drunkenly hovering over me with his flaccid cock in his hand? Tapping me on the face with it till he became enraged with his own impotence?

That was when the beatings usually started. The only silver-lining I could find was that a fist to the side of the head seemed to sometimes work better than melatonin.

The stinging in my palms brought me out of the onslaught of

flashbacks threatening to take over. I looked up and my hand was raised. My palm open and ready to slam down onto Micheal's now very red and swollen face as the realization of where I was slowly crept into my consciousness. I was straddling the chest of my now-dead ex-husband, the father to my son, abuser or not. And I felt every ounce of my stomach twist up.

Like a spring-loaded trap, I leaped off Micheal and, lacking any balance, staggered towards the kitchen sink. Making the mistake of looking off into the living room. My eyes instantly fell on the gruesome remains of Danielle lying on Brian's stomach, both of their heads unrecognizable. Hers was a mess of bone and minced meat, the shotgun having painted the wall behind her with red-and-pink chunks of flesh. Brian's head, on the other hand, was mostly intact. More so resembling what I remembered Humpty-Dumpty looking like after he'd fallen off the wall.

Oh, fuck!

I threw myself over the kitchen sink, my arms framing the sides of the rectangular basin. I slapped the faucet handle up just in time to begin dry-heaving and then succeeded, *to my dismay and pleasure,* in getting sick. Every bit of what I'd had and didn't have in my belly violently came up.

In just a few days' time, I'd finally ridden myself of my boogeyman. Lost practically every friend I'd made in the last year and the man who I had fallen in love with, the one I saw a future with. But I wasn't going to cry. I refused to cry.

32

SERA

I fucking hated crying in front of people. Ever since I was a child, I hated it. So much so that when I was in trouble, got hurt, or my kitten got run over by the neighbor's vehicle, I bit my lip. I never allowed myself to cry, 'cause Daddy said not to.

"What the bloody hell are you crying about, Sera Doll?" he'd said from as early as I could remember.

I'd been so excited to ride my bicycle without the training wheels for the first time. Daddy stood at the bottom of the hill we'd decided on together for my first big ride. He had his massive VHS recorder on his shoulder like one of those green toy soldiers my big brother had when he was alive. I never met him or anything, but I'd sneaked into his room a few times.

Brother had been on the 1988 Pan Am Flight that blew up over Scotland on its way to the United States of America. He'd gone with our nan to audition for a Broadway show. Daddy had never approved of John's theatrical flair or nan's and mum's insistence he pursue a life in the arts. He'd wanted John to follow in his footsteps and become a Royal Marine, a Sergeant, not a *Modern Major General*. Brother was not the sort for rugby or football, though, it seemed.

When John died, and I was born a few years later, my mum might have named me Sera. But in his mind, my dad must have named me Samuel. Nan had been on that flight with him, and when mum lost them both in one bang, her heart couldn't take it. Or at least that's what I believed, because she died giving birth to me. My daddy, though, there wasn't a day he didn't treat me like a boy. And by age fourteen, he was beating me like a man, telling me if it wasn't for my birth, mum would still be alive.

But the day my breasts were too developed for him to ignore anymore was the same day he'd staggered into my bedroom drunk. Holding his quail gun in one hand and personal bottle of brandy in the other, he'd paused to glare at me.

It wasn't his actual personal brand. He just liked feeling important.

"You sorry excuse for a son! Daddy's Sera Doll," he cursed, throwing the bottle at me. Only to miss and smash the bottle against the wall. The explosion of glass and its aftermath raining down on me had me shooting up in bed. I'd not slept with a shirt on that night. So when I sat up, bare to the world, I was horrified to see my father, bleary-eyed and stewed, wobbling in the doorway with his gun.

I'd never forget the scream. No, the cry *that led up to that shot. The one that painted my fourteen-year-old face with her drunken daddy's brains.*

He was so horrified, so against admitting he'd lost his actual son and produced a daughter in his place that he'd taken his own life.

That was what I called toxic masculinity, ladies.

It wasn't the men who wanted to open doors or chop firewood for you. It was the men so obsessed with their own cocks that they'd convinced themselves that what mattered most was their last name. But I still needed—still *wanted*—a daddy, and I'd lost the only one I had. Worst of all, part of me felt like it was my fault.

My adoptive parents were great, of course. They treated me like their own and loved Alex from the moment he was born. But it would never erase the trauma I'd suffered or the feeling that I was never good enough for my birth father.

I'd only told that to one person in my life. My late husband, Micheal, during a night of intimacy and vulnerability. The first time he and I got into a serious fight, however, he'd called me his *"Sera Doll."*

It was an intentional slap to the face. Micheal knew that and exploited it. Eventually, it became his whip.

33

SERA

Asplash of the cold water on my face brought me back to the here and now. I grabbed the dish towel hanging on the front of the stove and used it to dry my face, watching intermittently as my sickness vanished down the drain. I stood upright and closed my eyes as I tried to focus on the noise of the world around me.

There was nothing. Not so much as a howl or a chirp of a cricket from the outside. Maybe the only useful thing I'd committed to memory from my daddy was that when a predator was near, the prey were silent.

The hairs on the back of my neck stood on end as I slowly placed the dish towel down and reached for the large Lamson's Chef Knife, *the Michael Myers knife*, drawing it from the block. Then I stepped out of the kitchen, leaving the sink running while doing my best not to make a sound, as my eyes flicked to the base of the stairs. Where I'd left Micheal.

It was entirely empty. Shotgun and all.

Fuck, why didn't I pick up the gun? Stupid fucking Sera.

I crept over to where he had been and looked around for any clue as to where he might have gone. But before I was able to decide on my next move, the wall behind me erupted into splinters.

"Fucking cunt!" Micheal's coarse voice sent a shock to my soul.

I spun towards the source and found him in the living room. Tucking the shotgun between his legs with one hand and attempting to rack the action to chamber the next round. His opposite hand was still bent at an unnatural angle, looking like something from *The Goonies*. More monster than human.

I rushed him. I didn't know what possessed me to do it, but at that moment, I felt it was my only option. So I charged at him with every ounce of strength I had left in my body, my knife at the ready. There was no stealth. No quiet approach. I was a mad beast.

He looked up, dropped the shotgun to the floor, and reached for the revolver still tucked in his waist just before my shoulder collided with him. The gun flew through the air and then spun away on the floor as he fell backwards. Taking me with him. I tucked my head down into my shoulders to defend myself from the onslaught of punches I was certain were coming. But didn't.

Something warm and wet was flowing over my hand and pooling between my fingers. And I could feel him struggling beneath me. His breathing strained. Like he was drowning. Daring to look down where I'd been holding the knife, I realized the majority of it was now embedded in Micheal's belly. All twelve inches.

Perhaps coming out of the shock of being stabbed, he tried to push me off him, but with each attempt, a new gush of blood flowed out over my hand. I watched, mesmerized as the stream changed direction and slowly ran over the tiny rose I'd tattooed on my pointer finger. I'd done it one day when I had too much time on my hands at the shop.

Maybe I should add some red ink to it. It's so pretty.

Fuck, why was I having this inner dialogue right now? Was I in shock?

A hand gripped the back of my head, yanking it up and then back down again, his forehead crashing into my nose. The crunching snap telling me he'd just shattered it.

"Bitch!" I cried out, one hand instinctively shooting to my nose as I pushed myself up, my hand on the knife faltering and giving him the opening he needed.

Leaning on his damaged palm, he swiped me to the side, back far enough for him to slam his boot into my chest. The force sent me flying backwards, into the end table beside Jade's body, my head cracking against the top edge and making my vision blur.

The next thing I knew, I was staring up at the beautiful rafters above me. Watching them move across the ceiling. A sudden and painful change in the surface beneath my head snapped me to reality as I was dragged over the kitchen's stone floor. I still couldn't focus my eyes but I could tell that's where we were. Micheal's voice was muffled while the scent of gas filtered through the stronger scent of copper in my busted nose.

"You always were a stupid bitch, you know. I could tolerate that, but you've become truly evil and vindictive. I was so good to you."

What was that clicking noise? Why did I smell gas?

"Then, without any provocation, you attacked me. Stole my dear child from my life and painted me the monster."

I slowly raised my head, ensuring that I was still in one piece before daring to look in the direction of the mysterious clicking noise. Micheal was standing in front of the gas stove, trying to light one of the burners.

If I'd had the energy, I might have laughed at the sight. Micheal had never shared in the household's daily tasks. He'd mowed the lawn and took out the trash, but that had been it. Anything inside the home that was not in the category of fixing or building was strictly *women's work.* Laundry, dusting, vacuuming, dishes, and of course cooking were some of my most-sacred duties, he'd say. My way of showing him respect for putting a roof over my and Alexander's head. I'd also been extremely fortunate to have a husband such as him, so that I hadn't been forced to pursue my own career. Despite the fact I'd been dreaming of becoming a tattoo artist since I'd been a teenager, and had secretly purchased my own machine to practice on fake skin with.

All this to explain that this was quite possibly the man's first attempt to use a stove.

A bright flash drew my focus back. "There we fucking go," he said as he held a short, broad knife over the flame.

I followed the length of his torso to see the larger knife still protruding from his body, while a loud clank told me he'd set the other blade directly onto the metal coil of the burner. He then held what appeared to be a pill bottle to his mouth, pouring its contents inside before washing it down with some alcohol. Tossing it onto the stone floor between us as soon as he was done.

The bottle shattered, spraying me and the area around me with various-sized shards of glass. My hands shot up, successfully shielding my face from being cut up while also reminding me of the wound on my shoulder.

"Fuck, Micheal!" I screamed, but before I was able to say more than that, I was cut off by the bark of his laughter.

He was fucking laughing. And it was the most sinister sound I'd ever heard. Like a massive ball of ice exploding against my ears. Then, in the blink of an eye, his uninjured palm gripped the handle of the knife I'd sank into his belly and tossed it onto the floor next to what remained of the bottle.

If I thought it looked like a Michael Myers's knife before, it definitely did now that it was coated in his blood.

His laugh became more strained, turning into a pained, grunting noise. And my eyes widened when I realized why. He'd picked up the blade from the burner and was now pressing the side of the heated metal over where I'd stabbed him.

He was cauterizing the wound to prevent himself from bleeding out. Bastard.

Realizing too late the opportunity he'd given me, I attempted to stand, only to be shoved back down when his boot hit my shoulder. *I hadn't even noticed him close the distance.* I landed on my side, catching myself on my forearms. I bit back tears when my arm slammed onto the stone. My only saving grace was the fact my body had shielded this part of the floor from becoming covered in glass.

Before I could sit up, I was tugged backwards. Micheal fighting to get my sweatpants down while yanking on the waistband at my hips.

"Stop fucking fighting it, you whore. Just like the good ol' days," he cursed, standing and using one hand to struggle with his belt and trousers till they'd fallen down to his ankles.

My eyes locked on to his as his words hit me. I raised myself up on my elbows to glare at him, ignoring the fact my pants were half down my ass. "Fuck you, you small-dicked arsehole."

I maintained eye contact as we each reached for two very different things. As he began petting his flaccid cock, my hand fished around the floor till it found what I'd hoped it would.

Micheal dropped onto his knees, one leg pressed against each side of me while his forearm dug against my throat. "You're going to regret saying that when I shove my massive cock into your dead ass—rigor mortis tightens everything up."

He smiled down at me, his saliva forming a long disgusting drop that hit my cheek, at the exact same time I watched his eyes change from delighted to horrified.

I pulled my hand back, producing the concealed chunk of glass I was still clutching, and quickly grabbed his fist, which was still gripping his hardening dick. Preventing him from releasing it as I pulled him towards me. I smiled up at him, despite the lack of oxygen in my brain, and brought the broken shard down between our hands and his groin. The moment I felt his warm skin begin to give way beneath the glass, he screamed louder and higher than I thought any male could. Pushing himself up from my neck as he flailed at me with his free arm.

The glass wasn't as sharp as the knife I'd stabbed him with earlier and it definitely required more of a sawing motion, but it did the trick. I could feel the resistance slowly diminish as glass cut through muscle, his urethra, and then came out the other side. It wasn't until that moment that I released my grip on his wrist.

His face was whiter than a sheet as he fell backwards, his hands going down to where blood was spurting out of him, just above where his testicles hung. I sat up, dropped the chunk of glass, and plucked the small bloody penis off the floor before getting to my knees. As I watched him rock side to side, I felt every horrible nightmare he'd created pour over me at once and quickly grabbed for the knife with my free hand. Positioning myself on top of him.

Something I hadn't willingly done since we'd met.

His face was a mix of rage, pain, and I had to guess fear as he glared up at me. Like Anakin looking up at Obi-Wan Kenobi at the end of *Revenge of the Sith*. All that was missing was—

"You fucking whore, fuck you!" he screamed at me.

Close enough.

"Fuck yourself, Mike!" I said, slapping the palm of my hand

over his face as I forced his own bloody, flaccid cock into his mouth. "Be a good boy and swallow."

My other hand glided the blade across his throat, then sheathed it back in his gut. He gagged and convulsed beneath me for a bit, but the more blood that flowed from his neck and groin, the less he moved. Till he stopped altogether.

"Sera."

34

The thick, metallic scent of blood was strong in the room, Mike's body still lying on the kitchen floor in a pool of crimson. He'd stopped convulsing some time before I'd stepped forward, making myself known to Sera.

I'd watched her fight back with everything she had. Watched her cut the bastard's dick off and shove it into his mouth.

I paused just a few feet away, not wanting to scare her. "Sera," I said as I dropped my mask and tossed my axe into the growing pool of blood at my feet.

She looked up at me like a kid seeing fireworks on the Fourth of July for the first time. And before I knew it, her arms were wrapped around my torso, squeezing me tighter than I'd ever been hugged before. My eyes broke from the pool of blood and shattered glass to look down at Sera. She trembled against me, but she wasn't crying. She was likely still on an adrenaline high from fighting him off.

The bastard must have thought I was dead and came to make his final move. My little harpy's claws were sharp, though. She'd fought back and won. I couldn't be more proud of her. Or more turned on. My erection began fighting my pants as it pressed up against her stomach, and I knew she felt it too.

"It's over, Sera. You did so good."

She peered up at me, her dark hair falling back, and suddenly my eyes were drowning in brilliant pools of obsidian. Without a word, she rose on her toes for a kiss. Soft at first. The combination of our full lips a loving embrace. Then, like a sudden storm, she was biting and tugging at my mouth as her hands ripped her blood-soaked hoodie up over her head. It fell to the floor with a wet smack, revealing her blood-stained Sullen Art brassiere. I grabbed her wrist when she tried to remove it.

"No… let me…" I said as I took in my feral harpy.

Stepping away from her, I leaned over Mike's body with a smile, patting him on the cheek once before yanking on the large kitchen knife my girl had plunged into his abdomen.

"You don't mind, do you?" I chuckled as I moved back to Sera. I turned the knife in my hand and noticed the way her eyes lit up with excitement and curiosity.

There was something in her expression I'd never seen before, as if she'd truly been awakened. Unleashed. Like a phoenix rising from the ashes. Not taking my focus off her, I hooked a finger under her brassiere and pulled it out just enough to slip the blade between her skin and the strip of cloth. With a slow slice towards me, the bra fell apart, revealing her perfect, porcelain, perky breasts. Returning the gesture, she proceeded to lift my shirt over my head. She winced when she spotted the three large black bruises from the shots I'd taken earlier.

"Oh my god," she muttered under her breath, brushing a hand over the discolored skin.

"No need to worry about me, baby girl. You're the one who actually got shot, it seems," I said, recognizing the injury to her shoulder.

I'd had to take a nasty fall down the hill to sell the illusion that he'd killed me—*though I'd actually lost consciousness for some time*—which wasn't hard. Body armor or not, getting shot fucking hurt. If Mike were a smart man, he'd have made sure the job was done. Then again, if he were a smart man, he wouldn't have followed my girl to America.

Once I'd been certain he was gone, I'd fought my way back up to the cabin, my body protesting the entire way. In addition to the nasty blows I'd taken, I was certain I'd broken a rib or two during the fall. That all had to wait. My girl had needed me. When I'd reached my truck, I'd cursed under my breath at the sight of all four tires flattened to the rims and my windshield smashed in.

Come on, still be there…

I'd prayed to myself as I carefully opened the back door and searched for my gear. "Fuck yes!" I'd exclaimed, tucking my holstered Glock 23 into the back of my pants and pulling out my go-bag.

And that all brought me to here. In the kitchen with my harpy. A chef knife clutched in my palm.

I looked down at the smooth, rather thick handle and an idea occurred to me, inspired by one of our mutually favorite books. Leaning over, I stabbed the knife down into Micheal's chest, giving it a light wiggle to ensure it was secure enough between his ribs. Then I smirked at Sera, lowering her pants the rest of the way before pointing at the protruding knife handle.

"Sit on it," I commanded, and watched her eyes light up all over again.

She began kissing and biting down on my tattooed chest, my black nipple barbells matching the ones she wore. Then, straddling Mike's body as well as the growing pool of blood, she unzipped my pants, the weight of my Glock clipped to the back of my belt taking them down quickly. My cock sprung out, a starved beast with its chains just undone.

My harpy wasted no time. Her blood-stained hand wrapped around my girth, her fingertips never meeting her thumb. All while I watched her slowly lower her honey-sweet core down onto the knife handle. Up and down, she stroked me from hilt to tip, as she began to ride the knife protruding from her dead ex-husband.

She was smearing blood all over. Not that I gave a fuck. My right hand gathered her hair into a tight ponytail as she began to lick and suck the tip. I wanted to see my girl swallow every inch of my cock.

I would raise hell for this woman. Die for this woman. I'd hunted this woman across the world. I'd killed for her. I worshipped her, and she worshiped me.

My head arched back and I let out a growl as she took my full length as deep as she could. About halfway. The harder she sucked my cock, the more intensely she ground on the knife. Once I felt the end of her throat meet my tip, I pushed down on her head, making her gag, her drool spitting out around my shaft.

"That's my good girl. Fuck, little harpy. I'm so proud of you."

As if to drive my words home, I thrusted into her mouth, enjoying the way she gagged each time but didn't try to pull away. My free hand reached down to pinch off her nose. I felt myself getting closer. *Fast.* Something about seeing my girl like this had gotten me so hot for her. More than usual.

"Fuck, baby girl… You want my cum?" I growled.

She hardly had the opportunity to respond, as I continued fucking her mouth until my cock erupted. She swallowed and took down all my cum, choking as her air ran out. And I withdrew my cock, a drop of my cum falling from my tip and onto Mike's expressionless face. A moment later, Sera's body tensed, relaxed, and tensed again as she came on the knife.

"Oh my… fuck!" she gasped as she quickly raised herself off the handle.

Sera coughed, the aftermath of my orgasm landing on the

edges of her lower lip as she gasped for air. Smiling at her, I reached down to run my thumb along her mouth and collect the droplets before slipping it past her lips. She sealed them tightly around the digit, her tongue circling as she gathered the last of my cum.

"That's the first time I've ever come with him," she said breathlessly.

I instantly wanted to correct her. Tell her she came with me. *Mike's corpse was just a prop in this scene. But I didn't want to ruin the moment.*

"That's my girl," I praised, as I guided her to her feet. Lifted her up and set her ass on top of the island bar we'd all prepared dinner on just a few nights before.

Sliding my hands back up over the outside of her thighs, I gripped her hips and shimmied her back from the edge. Then I hooked my right foot onto the leg of the nearby bar stool, pulled it towards me, and sat down in front of my special meal.

Guiding her heels up to the counter's edge, nice and wide, I took a moment to admire my girl. She was still a little swollen from our previous encounters but I could tell she was so wet and hot for me right now. In the light, I could see that she was glistening, her slit appearing to sparkle like morning dew in a rose garden. Her thighs displayed dark blue bruises from our repeated encounters over the last few days.

I drew her closer, my mouth watering and my jaw aching while the aroma of her arousal washed over me like fresh honeysuckles.

"Fuck…" I growled out, trying to restrain myself.

Wishing to savor the moment, I kept my lips a mere inch away, breathing her in. I'd never done drugs before. But I imagined that the feeling I got when I was this close to my girl's warm, sweet honey—what it did to me—was probably the kind of high junkies dreamed of achieving.

I kissed her softly, the wetness of her passion making a light smacking sound, like the first drop of rain into a still lake. That one kiss was all it took before I was on her. Needed her. Craved her. Unable to go another minute, I ran my tongue up the soft and delicate lips of her forbidden fruit.

Forbidden to all but me.

My hands hooked around the outside of her thighs, my fingers gripping tightly as my tongue focused on her sensitive bud and began its dance. Her breathing grew harder and faster, the rise and fall of her chest mirroring her growing pleasure.

"James, fuck," she whimpered as she adjusted from resting on her palms to leaning back on her forearms.

My girl was high right now. She'd never killed before. In a few hours, the week's events that all led to this night—to Mike's lifeless body on the kitchen floor—would hit her like a bomb. I needed to provide her as much of a cushion as possible.

It wasn't long before I could feel her growing closer to a climax. I was having to swallow the evidence of her arousal more frequently.

"Fuck, don't sto…" she cried out as her legs trembled, and suddenly my mouth was filled with a spray of hot passion. Sealing my lips around her, I drank her in as my tongue continued its intense caress of her delicate bud till her body settled, and I knew she was done.

"What a messy girl you are. Don't worry, I'll always be here to clean up after you now." I smiled up at her. Then I pushed to my full height, my arms hooking under her thighs and pulling her a little closer to the edge.

I didn't need to do anything else. She reached down between her legs and guided the head of my length inside her ready core.

In this moment, my girl didn't need something soft and sensual. She needed to be fucked. So that's what I did.

Gripping her thighs tightly, I thrusted into her, the wet sound of skin on skin slapping together echoing in the night's silence.

"Fuck!" she screamed on the second or third thrust, as I

increased my artillery barrage, like an assault on her insides with my hardened length. Her arms reached up to hug around my neck, her breath hot against my cheek as I laid into her.

With each thrust I delivered, I felt my breath shortening, a side effect of either the ribs I was certain were broken or the internal bruising from being shot three times. I couldn't tell which.

Realizing I needed to change things up to maintain the momentum, I strengthened my grip around her legs and took a careful step back, avoiding slipping in the large amount of blood at my feet. Then I carried her off towards the living room. Lifting and dropping her back onto my shaft as we went. She matched my rhythm, pulling herself up and down until we reached the couch.

I plopped onto the seat beside Jade, ignoring a glass of what looked like wine tipping over with the force. The springs added an extra bounce, causing me to thrust deeper as Sera came back down onto me. Neither of us batted an eye at the fact there was a corpse beside us. Sera ground and bounced on my cock like her life depended on it. Like she was running from the events of the last few days, right to me.

I gripped her hips and followed her rhythm, pulling her down harder when she lowered herself onto me. Every smack of our bodies seemed to mimic the lightning from last night's storm. One of her hands moved from my shoulders to the front of my throat, her nails sinking into my skin.

A sudden violent tug of my hair yanked my head back against the couch. Sera's hips taking on a whole new rhythm. Something faster and much more intense. I shifted my hands up from her hips to squeeze and massage her breasts. But the moment my eyes drifted down from her face to admire her chest, she seemed to growl. *Like an enraged harpy.*

"No, I need to look into your eyes!"

Surprised by her ferocity, I snap my eyes back up to hers. She looked *absolutely feral.*

We both lost control, our bodies tensing and shuddering as we released all the tension, fear, rage, sorrow, and love we'd built up. Leaving our nightmare and entering a moment of pure bliss. Our chests were heaving by the end as we each tried to catch our breath.

"What do we do now?" she asked between shallow pants.

"We stay here. Someone is going to come searching for that sheriff. Or once the power comes back on, we can call for help. Either way, I'm sure someone will come soon, Harps. Don't worry. You're safe now," I said as I gently caressed her back with a blood-stained hand.

"I love you, James."

"I love you too, Harpy."

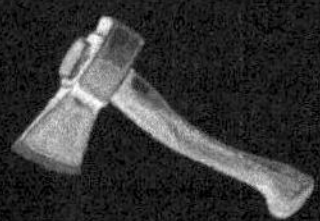

Fire, Ma, Pa, blood, screaming, gunshots, Robert, Lyndsey, Jade, Danielle, Brian, KingArthur—no, Micheal, and Sera…

I woke up to red-and-blue flashing lights on the walls around me. I was still in the cabin. In the living room. Two deputies shining a light in my eyes as a paramedic attempted to lift Sera off me.

We were both covered in blood.

I couldn't make out what they were saying. My mind was too focused on wrapping my arms around Sera tighter. *No one was going to take her from me!* Then I saw the color of her skin. She seemed paler than usual, her lips losing their lush hue.

"It's okay, James. You'll always find me again," she whispered while smiling down at me.

She needed help. Her shoulder wound must have been

worse than I'd thought. I allowed the paramedics to take her from me. I was too weak to carry her anyway. It was quite possible that the broken ribs had punctured something internally, which could amount to much worse troubles. However, when I tried to stand, I was held down by one of the deputies.

"Hey, it's okay, buddy. Let's just take it easy. The next set of paramedics is coming for you. You're both going to be okay," he said in a tone that betrayed what I was certain were meant to be calming words.

Suddenly, the thought of not being able to see Sera sent a flood of white-hot rage through my body. I could feel it pulsing in my eyes. My right fist collided with the side of the first deputy's head, my free hand unholstering the duty weapon from his hip. But before I could get a shot off, something pressed against my temple and an electrical current surged through me.

Then all the lights were gone.

EPILOGUE

SERA

Having just arrived home from the tattoo shop, I'd gone straight to the kitchen to warm up the leftovers James had told me were in the fridge. I grabbed the covered plate of pulled pork, mashed potatoes, and asparagus, placing it in the microwave and hitting the *two* button.

Then I wrapped my arms around my chest as I recalled the tattoo I'd done today. A Michael Myers style kitchen knife. Each time I'd wiped at my client's skin and smeared the blood, I'd flinched. I shouldn't be surprised by the tattoo choice, though. It was the week before Halloween, after all, and exactly two years since Shingletown.

When the authorities had finally finished questioning us about what James and I had taken to morbidly calling the *Unsubscribing at Masktok Cabin*, we'd taken some time to heal before beginning to plan for the future. Construction on the main home of his ranch had already started, and he still had a large sum of money left over from the insurance claim. So, in place of a ring, he'd proposed to me with the title to a piece of real estate. A spot that would become my very own tattoo shop. *Morphine Kiss Tattoo* was located just under an hour's drive from the ranch and was in a rather ideal location.

I wish I could say I'd been the one to design the interior, but I'd have been lying. James had pieced it together near perfectly with a gothic *boutique theme. It was also likely the only tattoo shop/dark romance library.* The waiting room was slightly larger than what you'd expect at a tattoo shop. And upon entering, after being greeted by my new apprentice Kearsten, you would be transported to the finest mini dark romance library Texas had ever seen. Somewhere that allowed you to rent a good book, for a small fee, and maybe even get a new tattoo when you returned it.

Pulling my meal out of the microwave, I caught the way the sunlight reflected on the large diamond on my left finger and smiled as I moved to my favorite spot in the kitchen. I stood beside the sink and looked out the window to watch the sun setting in the West Texas sky while humming "Lullaby" by The Spill Canvas.

It was the first song we'd danced to as husband and wife.

James had let me have the majority of the say in the reconstruction of the ranch's main house after it had burned down a month or two prior to our Booktok group's nightmare of a vacation. The same fire he'd tragically lost his parents in. He'd shown me photos of what it used to look like. A beautiful two-story Birmingham. I'd mentioned how I wanted the kitchen to be on the west side of the house, so that I could look out and see the sunset behind the lovely hill where his family plot rested.

It was the perfect blend of beauty and spooky if you asked me.

Everything else, however, I wanted exactly as his parents loved it—with the addition of two extra rooms. James didn't know this yet, but our little family was getting a new member soon.

Despite all the good in our lives now, I still had nightmares from time to time. Nights where I'd wake up without the ability to move my body. All my friends dead around me. I'd always wake up to James cradling me in his arms, brushing my hair, and rocking me back and forth. Telling me that everything was going to be okay.

"Mum!" A bright, youthful voice had me turning to see Alexander enter the kitchen and make straight for the biscuit jar on the counter.

"Alexander! No, sir!" I scolded as his hand lifted the top of the jar.

"Ah, let the boy have a cookie, Harps. He's earned it! Haven't you, killer?"

I heard the gravelly base before he entered the room, and my heart fluttered just like it did every time I saw him. James filed in behind Alexander, reaching into the jar and handing my son a biscuit without waiting for my response.

"Go on then. Wash up for bed, kiddo," James urged, and we both watched as Alexander double-hand grabbed the biscuit, bit into it, and sprinted off.

"Love you, Mum! Love you, James!" he called out as he fled the kitchen with his prize.

My eyes darted up to the man standing in front of me, his forest-green eyes like a mental aloe vera cooling my burning temper. "You spoil him."

"Nonsense. The boy not only helped me feed the hogs, he also mucked two of the stalls and rode Zip bareback." James smirked, but he'd lost me at the mention of the three-year-old colt he'd only recently broken.

"You did not!" I scolded him.

"I did, and he did. You should be proud, Harps. The boy is going to make a fine ranch hand one day." James smiled as he closed the distance between us.

I maintained my stern expression for as long as I could. But the moment those large, tattooed arms closed around me, I melted like butter. Looking up to him, I gave one last attempt at a glare before I caved. "You're so good with him. Thank you."

James shook his head, kissed me on the forehead, and patted my back before slapping me on the ass. "He's a really good kid, Sera. Deserves a good dad, and I love him as if he were my own."

"I know you do, and I'm grateful to you." I smiled, kissing him back on his bearded jaw.

"You ready for our trail ride in the morning, Harps? I've got our packs all set to go, and Kearsten will be here at sunrise to watch over Alex." James kissed me a final time before stepping over to the kitchen and pulling a can of Budweiser out, cracking it open and taking a long drink.

"You better be paying that girl!" I cast him a threatening look, waving the fork in my hand for emphasis before popping a piece of pork into my mouth.

My man could cook.

"Of course I'm paying her. Don't worry about it, Harps. You just make sure your feral ass is ready in the morning. We're setting out before sunrise," he said as he followed the same path Alexander had taken a few moments ago. "Hey, kiddo, how about an episode of our show before bed!" he yelled out, and then I heard the sound of his boots bounding up the stairs.

Over the past few months, it was like James had been reliving his own childhood by showing Alexander all of his favorite cartoons. The current series? *Gargoyles.* It melted my heart to watch my child and my man-child bonding.

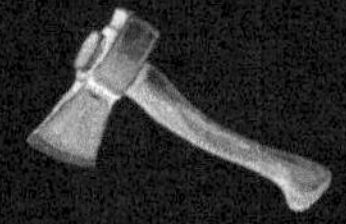

The next morning, I learned that *before sunrise* really meant *two hours* before sunrise. Thankfully, James had the foresight—and likely the strong sense of self-preservation—to wake me up with coffee in hand. He'd been fully dressed, cowboy hat and all. He'd let his beard grow out since we moved to Texas, abandoning the clean, trim appearance he'd sported when we first met. Now he looked like a taller, tattooed Bradley Cooper.

And here I'd thought he couldn't get any more attractive.

"Well, good morning, cowboy. Here to take me away?" I smiled while referencing one of my favorite country songs.

Stepping into the horse barn, I was not surprised to see that both our Friesians were saddled up and ready to go, just like he said they'd be. Midnight, my mare, and Fury, his stallion, were both tied up in their respective stalls. They were kind of our wedding presents to ourselves. Between James's parents' life insurance and the money I surprisingly received after Micheal's passing—*it seemed he'd forgotten to remove me as his benefactor when we'd divorced*—we had a very nice nest egg to rest on while we got the ranch back into proper order.

Nearly an hour later, James and I were well into our trail ride, much like the ones he'd take me on while we video-chatted. It was a live-action retelling of what we both considered our first date when he'd taken me along for the entire ride one morning. We'd watched the sun rise together, each amazed by the reality that as his sun was just rising, mine was at its peak— though hidden behind the typical dreary sky.

The majority of the six-hundred acre ranch was flat land. However, part of it, especially near the Rio Grande, included the Sierra Blanca mountains, which was exactly where we were headed. We spent most of the ride making small talk or pointing out the various wildlife around us while enjoying the rhythmic squeaking of the leather of the saddles. When we reached one of the taller eastern mountains over the river, James dismounted and pulled two metal stakes from his saddle bag as well as a mallet.

"My parents used to come up here a lot. It's actually where my dad proposed to Mama." He hammered one of the stakes into the ground, then hooked a long rope to the bottom of Fury's bridle and secured it to the stake. After repeating the process with Midnight, he guided me down. "May not look like much, but it's magical at the right time of day," James said, releasing my hand and pulling the bed roll off the back of my saddle.

"I can imagine. The sun isn't even up yet, and I think it's lovely up here," I said, stepping farther south, over to where I could peer down at the Rio Grande, Mexico just on the other side.

"Careful, baby girl. Make sure you watch your footing 'round here. Besides a nasty fall, you wouldn't want to disturb a sleeping rattler," he said from behind me, laying out the bed roll before grabbing a second one from his saddle and placing it on top.

"Fuck's sake," I cursed out, thankful that he'd been too preoccupied with the bedding to see me jump at the mention of rattlesnakes. I'd yet to have a close encounter with one of those terrifying creatures, but the day I found a Texas tarantula in the bed, James had to fight me for hours to keep me from burning the main house down for a second time.

The sky was growing brighter, a mix of brilliant orange and reds, reflecting on the river below that seemed to wind and bend for eternity.

"Come lie down, Harps."

I heard James's smokey voice from behind me. I hadn't even realized I'd zoned out. Turning back towards him, I went to accept his hand. Only to pause and start stripping off my clothes until I was standing bare in front of him. Then I took his still outstretched palm in mine.

He tried to guide me to his side, but I drop to my knees

between his legs instead. Casually skimming my hands along his waist as I undid his belt and jeans before pulling them down. I smiled as I watched his length jump to attention. Ready for me. Not wishing to waste any more time, I leaned forward and ran my tongue from base to tip. Taking the entirety into my mouth while ensuring it was properly lubricated before shoving him down and quickly climbing on top of him.

I felt every inch of my cowboy—my hero—enter my core, his length penetrating me all the way to the hilt. "I want to put a baby inside you, baby girl," he groaned as I started to slowly grind my hips.

"You already have, Daddy." I wrapped my legs around his torso. I didn't give him the opportunity to lift his arms, pinning them to his sides, his fingers just barely scratching my ass.

The sensation of his cock throbbing inside me sent an electrical current through my body, and all I wanted was *more*. James groaned with pleasure beneath me as I took charge, my movements as feral as any predator in these mountains.

Primal lust drove me to grind my hips more ferociously. His eyes pierced into mine, daring me onward, so I gripped the sides of his head. Another surge of electricity coursed through my body, and I lunged forward, pressing my lips against his. My tongue forcing its way inside his mouth.

The moment I felt him erupt inside my trembling core, I too let go. As his climax neared its end and he entered the overly sensitive stage of an orgasm, James managed to break free from my hold on his head.

You need to stay still so I can finish! I screamed at him internally.

Managing to regain my grip, I pinned his head back and was rewarded as the current hit me once more. This time granting me the orgasm I'd been working so hard to achieve.

"Don't move, James. That's a good boy," I purred at him, my head casting a shadow over his face as the sun rose behind us.

EPILOGUE

JAMES

PRESENT

"More." *Sera.*

"I need you to stay still." *Sera.*

"Good boy." *Yes, Sera, I am.*

I can't fucking see!

My body isn't responding and I don't understand why. Trying to focus on my vision alone, I will every ounce of my strength to my eyes. I blink till my world slowly comes back into view. At first, all I can make out is the dark outline of Sera's head. Over me. Blocking out the brilliant Texas sun. She looks like the Mother Mary wearing a golden halo.

Sera.

The more I blink, the clearer everything becomes, and the more I realize the figure standing over me is *not* my Harps. It's a woman, but she's blond—at least from what I can tell from the strand of hair hanging loosely from her medical mask.

"I think that's it for now," the woman says, though her voice seems much more distant than it should be. She pats my chest. "James, you did very well today."

I want to respond. To yell: *Who the fuck are you? Where is Sera? And where am I?*

I want to, but I can't. The majority of my body is restrained and that includes the rubber bite guard filling my mouth. Feeling a surge of panic and rage, I struggle to gain my freedom.

"It's okay, James!" I hear that voice again, just before there's a sharp pinch in my neck. Not long after that, my eyes grow heavy.

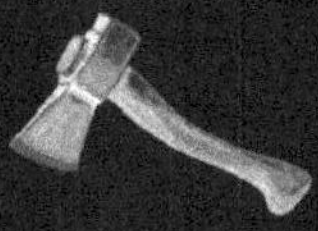

"James? Oh, come now, James. We aren't done yet. I need you," Sera says so softly.

I bury my face in my hands and rub at my eyes for a few seconds, before sitting up and staring at my palms in confusion. Sera is sitting in front of me, at the foot of our bed, with a bundle of pink cradled in her arms.

"Rose, your daddy is so sleepy. He works so hard to protect us."

I slowly push up and lean forward, smiling at her words. Rose is my pride and joy. I love Alexander as much as any father loves his son. However, without shame, I would openly tell any court in the land that I love my little Rose in a different, magical sort of way. It's my duty as a father of a princess.

"Nonsense, Harps. Let me hold her," I say, rising from my chair and beckoning for the product of our undying love.

Sera meets me halfway, transferring the pink bundle from her arms to mine. "Here you are, James."

I can feel the smile pulling at the corners of my lips as I hold my daughter to my chest and lower myself back into my seat. My eyes drift downward. Where, to my confusion, I see a thick red journal instead of a pink blanket.

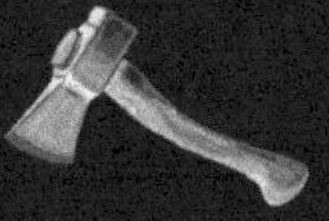

"What is this?" I say softly, not recognizing my own voice as I lean back in my chair. I lift one hand and massage my throat while the other opens the journal and starts to flip through the pages. Filled with my handwriting.

"It's your journal, James. We've been over this. It's where you keep all of your memories of what happened, of what happened two years ago, and we sort through them. So you can accept the truth."

My eyes shift from the journal in my lap up to the woman sitting across from me, a pen and pad on the desk in front of her.

"*What really happened?*" I clench my fingers around the binding of the journal. "*What really happened!* I know what really happened! None of you will listen to me!" I throw the journal across the desk, hitting some sort of decorative statue off the bookshelf behind her. Before I have the opportunity to do anything else, something hard collides with the side of my head.

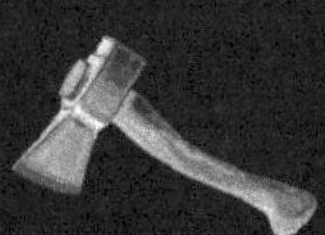

When I wake next, it's with a splitting headache. I slowly search my immediate surroundings with my hands and come to the conclusion I'm in a small bed. Opening my eyes confirms it, though.

"Still fucking here," I curse as I stand from the plain cot beneath me, my eyes dashing to the bunk above mine. Only comforted by the silver lining that at least they haven't tried to give me another roommate.

Not that I really suspected they would. Not since my last one ended up paralyzed from the waist down.

I step towards the desk where my journal sits, and a scent steals my attention. *Vanilla.* Lunging over to the small open window in the wall, I grip the bars, press my face as close as I can, and peer out.

My room here at the Villa de Psycho must be one of the best, because it comes with a view. I can see the entire 7-Eleven at the corner down the street. Except what I see now steals the air from my lungs.

Sera, wearing my brand's hoodie and sweatpants, just like that night two years ago. She's holding a pink bundle, Alexander standing at her side and grabbing on to her pants pocket. His eyes so full of pain as he grips a vintage Goliath action figure in his free hand.

Before I can call out her name, a large tractor trailer drives by, advertising the newest model of Ford Mustang. My teeth grit so hard together I'm certain one will crack.

Somehow, in the mere seconds it takes for that trailer to pass by, all three of them are fucking gone. My girls and my chosen son are out there, and I'm locked in here!

"Sera!" I scream until my throat bleeds. I scream until everything goes black again.

my name iS james i didn't want to writE
this stoRy but the doctors made me do it
they rAward me wIth Letting me have
mOre time in the library Very cool If
youirE reading this that means theY published
it and my friend snuck this intO the end
just like I bribed him to dU.

I do not know where i aM just that it is
psyChiatric hOspital prison Maybe they say I
have to write this toremember the real
story i kNow what happened thouCh.
MY HARPY is waiting for me out there i
will FIND her AGAIN

BONUS CHAPTER
ROBERT'S MURDER

"Stupid fucking hick-ass cowboy. Fucking cock block is what he is. Bitch-ass Texan. Fuck him!" I can hear him cursing and yelling as he approaches his car but he doesn't know I'm waiting for him. The hatch of the boot lets out a hiss as it opens but I remain perfectly still. He won't notice me. I'm certain of it. The entire car shakes as he tosses his luggage bag in and slams the boot shut. "Bastard wouldn't even let me grab my guitar. What does he even care if I fuck Lyndsey…bastard is fucking that British whore Sera." I flinch at that. How dare he speak like that about Sera. I grip the handle of the k-bar tighter.

Patience, I tell myself.

The driver's side door opens and the car shakes as the long-haired one called Robert drops into the driver's seat and he starts the vehicle up. From the darkness of the back seat, I watch him open the center console and pull a Ziploc bag of white powder from it. Reaching a small pocket knife inside he collects a small amount of the white power onto the blade and holds it up to his nose and snorts it, and then repeats the process with the other nostril. Shaking his head, he tosses the small knife into the passenger seat and puts the car in drive.

I sit as patiently as I can, despite his horrendous singing to an Eagles classic. I have to let him get a fair distance away from the cabin. It wouldn't do me right to kill him too close and risk anyone spotting the taillights going still. Once we have driven about five minutes worth of time away from the cabin, I act. Quietly, I lean forward and thrust the knife into his side right in between his ribs. A sharp gasp escapes him as he looks down to where my gloved hand holds the knife's handle against his side.

"What the fuck!" He screams, the sound of it breaking into a cry of terror. His hands turn the wheel sharp to the right and I hear the car's engine rev as his foot slams all the way down on the pedal. With my other hand, I grip the driver's seat in front of me and hold on tight, pressing my body into its back bracing myself. There is a loud crash and all momentum comes to a sudden stop as the car's front wraps around a tree along the side of the driveway. Robert, not wearing his seatbelt, is thrown forward, my knife tearing back through flesh as his body smashes against the steering wheel, the airbags either failing or not being present at all. The windshield having broken in the impact hangs down over the dash chunks of it scattered over the front seats. Sitting back in my seat, leaving my knife in his side, I take a moment to collect myself.

That could have been a bit smoother. I'll have to do better with the next one. I think to myself as I get out of the vehicle, having to kick the inside of my door to get it to open. Moving forward, I climb onto the hood of the car and crouch down so that I'm directly in front of him. I should be getting back to the party soon but I don't want to rush this too much.

Robert lifts his head slowly, a large gash now on his forehead from where it collided with the steering wheel.

"And that is why you should always wear a seat belt, Robert" I say but my voice comes out muffled and distorted from under the mask. His eyes blink slowly, trying to focus on me. Between the blow to the head and the blood loss, I don't expect him to be conscious for too long. Leaning forward through the front of the car I reach down and pull my knife back from his abdomen.

"James?" he asks slowly, struggling to hold his head up.

I reach the knife out and tap him on the nose. "You should have stayed away from my girl."

He shakes his head, the tears flowing down his face. "James! What man, I never touched Sera. I'm leaving. I'm sorry, please don't kill me." The last of his sentence comes out broken and drowned out by a mix of tears and running snot.

"Mustang, please." He sobs.

"Hush, Robert, I am going to give you a chance to live. I believe you are sorry and I am a gentleman after all." I set the knife down behind me on the hood and pick up two small pieces of broken glass one in each hand.

"Oh, my friend, you have something in your eyes. Here, allow me to assist you." My voice comes out slowly as I savor this final look in his eyes. Moving onto my knees, I lean slightly into the vehicle and grab the sides of his head, holding the pieces of glass between each thumb and forefinger.

I smile at him from underneath my mask as I suddenly press the glass into his eyes with my thumbs,grinding them into the soft of his eye sockets. Despite wearing thick leather gloves, I feel the moment his eyeballs pop, the vitreous oozing out and down his cheeks, like a water balloon filled with warm slime. His scream is bone chilling as my thumbs sink into his eyes just enough to ensure the glass is really in there, his face flooding with blood. I pull my hands back and grab one of his arms, using his sleeve to wipe the blood from my gloved hands. Panicked, he pulls both hands back to cover his face, muffling the sound of his screams. I jump off the hood of the car and with great effort get his driver side door open.

"If you can make it back to the main road, perhaps you will be able to find a way to the hospital. Do that and you get to live. Good luck, Robert," I sneered lowly from behind the mask.

He flops out of the car barely catching himself on his feet and stumbles off into the night, one hand holding his side while the other hovers out in front of him. "Oh, do watch for bears!" I yell after him.

Before turning to make my way to the party, I reach in and grab the mix of drugs from the center console. "These will come in handy later." I say to myself tucking them in the pocket of my trousers.

Giving Robert one last glance I turn and begin sprinting back towards the cabin. I'd already been gone too long.

3CROWS AUTHOR SERVICES

3Crows Author Services is a two woman team dedicated to making author services high quality and affordable. As authors themselves, they know the difficulty in trying to find a designer who will bring your vision to life and look after your book baby. It's their mission to help authors create the most perfect version of their book possible.

They offer services such as cover design (both premade and custom), interior formatting, graphic design, promotional materials and merchandise designs.

You can find them here:
https://www.linktr.ee/3crows.author.services

ACKNOWLEDGMENTS

This is where I'm supposed to get all emotional and say how I couldn't have done this without certain people. Thank my dad for nutting in my mom, and my mom for not swallowing me, right?

Well, fuck that. I did this because I'm a Leo and a Marine Corps Veteran.

Wait, I need to be humble? Oh, fuck, right. Got it. Now channeling Hawkeye Pierce from the "Chief Surgeon Who?" episode.

In all seriousness, if you are reading this, I want to thank you first and foremost. I thank you, because at the end of the day, there will be people who I think are close to me who will never read this book. Thank you to all the amazing readers, friends, narrators, and brave indie authors who took a chance on me.

I've made so many friends and a beautiful community on TikTok since October 2024. The backbone of that community being the OG team of moderators who have kept me in line and going—despite my madness—and continue to do so: *Antares, Ashtin, Nicole, Tsuna, Annie, and Rose.* Former Mods: *Belle, Katie, and Espookymami. Thank you all.*

Antares, I want to also thank you for the amazing character art you did for this book. I wasn't sure what to expect, but you blew everyone's mind with the incredible quality of your art! You are a true brother. Semper Fi!

In my short time on Booktok, I've had the honor and privilege to interview and meet amazingly brave and creative indie authors such as: *D. Raven, Ezra King, Ayden Perry, Sybil Knight, Pandora Cress, Kayleigh Hilton, SK Pryntz, AA Powers, and Mia Battaglia.* As well as work with others such as: *T.C. Weaver, Aria Devon, and the Boldrini Authors.* I consider each and every one of them dear friends and mentors to one degree or another. Each of them took time out of their days to talk to me on a live stream about their work and their journeys to become an author.

Additionally, I want to briefly thank my mentor and partner R.L. Hemm, who took me under her wing as a narrator and has constantly helped my career flourish without any personal motive. I'd also like to thank one of voice acting's current kings: Corvin King. Early on in my narration career, Mr. King took a good deal of time out of his day to answer many of my questions and offer very solid advice. In his words, *I figured you definitely deserve some time and I'm wishing you all the best.* Thank you for encouraging the little guy.

I want to extend a special thanks to what I've begun to call my Booktok UN. Dear friends and respected role models in the Booktok community: Maskedman96 <3 <3 <3 *(I'm going to save you!)*, SJ, Amy, Liv, JD, Laura, Sav, Jordan, Brandi, Sarah, Abby, Layla, Alix, Duchess.renee & BooksareSanctuary. You all have been there for me at one point or another, and I love you each for it.

@3crows.author.services on Instagram: You reached out to a random aspiring author with a dream and some drive, and here we are. Out of the pure kindness of y'all's hearts, you have helped inspire me, support me, and push me onward. The cover you put together for my book is mind-blowing. I hope one day soon to be able to pass on the kindness and love y'all have passed on to me.

Friend, mentor, author, *Sybil Knight*: Madame, once upon a time, you took a chance on a random masked man who wanted to steal you for an interview. Perhaps it was your sixth sense telling you to take pity on me because I'm a Marine but you did. *SKIN* is one of the small handful of books I've read in the last year that has encouraged me to push the boundaries. Since I've begun my own journey to claim the title of *indie author,* you have been my biggest supporter. In addition to promoting my content, you have not only answered all my random questions, but you've practically edited the entire book to the degree you are the Super Saiyan of alpha readers. I could never repay the kindness you've shown me.

Editor Kat Pagan: Madame, you saved my ass! I'd spoken to a few editors, but the schedules just weren't working. I panicked and am pretty sure I gained a few new white hairs in my beard. The work you have put into this book in the short amount of time may be a world record. Thank you so much for the dedication, professionalism, and skill you have shown while guiding my baby to its birth.

Finally, The Red Room Discord, my ARC readers: First of all, if we ever meet in a cabin in the middle of nowhere, I promise there will be no gore. You all took a chance with a debut indie author and a male author writing smut at that. I can never tell you how grateful I am for that. Thank you, not only for your support, but for growing friendships and a positive community. This is what Booktok is meant to be.

My love, *@Sarahs.books*: Sarah. Thank you for being my biggest supporter for nearly a full year now. You are my muse, fuel, and anchor. Since day one, you have encouraged me even when I wanted to quit. Seeing your excitement firsthand as you'd read one chapter or another kept me driven to go further. Your obsession with Lola's murder did something unspeakable to me… but I digress.

Not only did you encourage me to keep writing, despite my own self-doubts, but you inspired who I hope others will see as a strong female main character. To me, Sera is a strong mother—

one who beat the odds—because, at the end of the day, she simply had no other choice.

She is in charge of her life but has had to fight for it. She then chases her dreams, dreams that had been stolen from her. In the end, she is her own champion. The strong woman I hope my own daughters one day grow to be.

I love you, Sarah.

ABOUT THE AUTHOR

The most accomplishment or title Grayton D has achieved is that of father to his two beautiful daughters. A very close second to that, Grayton D is a proud Marine Corps veteran with almost eight years of service. It was during his first enlistment as a Field Artillery Cannon Crewman, that he discovered his passion for reading. Anytime the gunline was quiet, he could be found hiding in the back of the 7-ton or sitting in the cradle of the howitzer with his Paperwhite Kindle in its pink leather case.

Novels such as the *Noble Dead Saga* by Barb and J. C. Hendee, and the *Star Wars: Bane Trilogy* by Drew Karpyshyn were the worlds he would escape to when he needed a break. Jumping ahead to the end of 2023, following the recommendation from long-term friend Kearsten, he picked up *Hooked* by Emily McIntire, and that became his gateway drug to all this.

Since 2024, he has now made the jump from reader to audiobook narrator and now indie author. You can find a complete list of current and past projects as well as his socials through any of his links down below.

https://graytond.com
https://linktr.ee/GraytonD

Merch Shop:
https://grayton-shop.fourthwall.com

Stay feral.